DIGITAL DESIRE

FORTIS BOOK 8

MADDIE WADE

Digital Desire: Fortis Book 8
Maddie Wade

Published by Maddie Wade
Copyright © January 2019 Maddie Wade

Cover: Envy Creative Designs
Editing: Black Opal Editing
Formatting: Black Opal Editing

This is a work of fiction. Names characters places and incidents are a product of the author's imagination or are used fictitiously and are not to be construed as fact. Any resemblance to actual events organizations or persons—living or dead—is entirely coincidental.

All rights reserved. By payment of the required fees, you have been granted the non-exclusive non-transferable right to access and read the text of this eBook onscreen. Except for use in reviews promotional posts or similar uses no part of this text may be reproduced transmitted downloaded decompiled reverse-engineered or stored in or introduced into any information storage and retrieval system in any form or by any means whether electronic or mechanical now known or hereafter invented without the express written permission of the author.

First edition January © 2019 Maddie Wade

ACKNOWLEDGMENTS

Thank you to Linda and Black Opal Editing for working hard to get this book ready on time.

Huge thanks you to my beta readers, Greta, Deanna, Lindsey and Rowena. Your feedback and advice was invaluable.

To Charlene at Envy Designs, thank you for the gorgeous cover.

To the readers and reviewers and bloggers thank you for your support. I hope you enjoy Will's book and get some anwers to some of your questions. The reviews you leave are all welcome and so appreciated, I read every single one with a smile on my face.

My readers, you are why I do this. Your thirst for what I write keeps me typing and working to put out the stories you want to read. Your love for the characters keeps me pushing through when times get tough.

*This book is dedicated to Deanna Lang.
Thank you so much for kicking my butt when I needed it and making this book the best it could be.*

PROLOGUE

HER HEART BEAT FAST AS SHE LAY IN HER BED, THE COVERS PULLED UP TO her chin and listened. The sound when it came, as she knew it would, made her sigh. She had known ever since she'd seen the look in her sister's eyes as they ate dinner that night with their parents, that Madison was going to try and sneak out.

Madison was a few years younger than she was and was the wild, free-spirited one of the family according to their dad. She was the sensible older sister, always got good grades, never got in trouble but that was how she liked her life—ordered and predictable.

But she adored her baby sister and had accepted and relished the role of big sister. Ever since Madison was born, she had mothered her and looked out for her and now they were teenagers she covered for her and protected her, following her into trouble to make sure she stayed safe.

Throwing back the covers she moved to the window just as Madison's feet hit the ground at the bottom of the cherry tree. Swinging her legs out of the window, her trainers already on her feet, she climbed down the trellis that was nailed to the wall being careful not to damage the clematis that were her mother's pride and joy.

"What took you so long? Come on, Brey," her sister said using the nickname for her that had started as a toddler because she couldn't say Aubrey and had stuck. Aubrey loved it, but Madison was the only one that called her that. Despite being so different they were close.

"Sorry, I was trying not to get us caught," she replied sarcastically as they raced to their bikes that were parked at the back of the shed.

As the girls climbed on their bikes and peddled their way across the field to the farm two miles over Aubrey felt exhilaration pump through her veins.

The cold October air kissed her skin, her lungs filled with it, the scent of apples from the orchard heady and smelling of home. It was her favourite smell in the world, it reminded her of her mum's apple pie, and nights by the fire when her mum crocheted, and her dad dozed after a hard day at the hospital.

As a surgeon, her dad kept weird hours, so when he was home, she loved them all being together. Tonight was a rare night when they had done just that. Daddy had played scrabble with her and Madison, pride in his eyes when she beat him. At sixteen she was still daddy's girl. She always would be, and she wanted desperately to go into medicine like him.

Madison was more like their mum, her art spoke to her and she was good, maybe one day she would be famous. Aubrey thought she would be, her sister was like a shining star and burning so bright that she almost burned you if you got too close.

Dropping their bikes outside the barn, the girls giggled as they joined hands and ran into the barn where the party was taking place. Madison beamed a smile at her as they saw some friends from school. Aubrey nodded, and Madison dropped her hand before kissing her cheek.

"Love you, Brey," she said with a quick tight hug, her infectious spirit hard to contain.

"Love you too, brat, now go have fun for a bit. I don't want us out for too long."

"Always the good girl, Brey," Madison said with a soft look.

"Yeah well, someone has to keep your ass in check," she replied brushing it off.

Aubrey walked to the long table that had been set up at the end of the barn as music played loudly. They were in the middle of nowhere, so nobody would hear it. She was pouring herself a coke when she felt someone beside her. She looked up into the most handsome face she had ever seen.

Tall, dark-haired, and with the most expressive brown eyes she had ever seen, but it wasn't that which made her heart stop beating. It was the cheeky, sexy, devilish grin he wore as he looked at her.

Taking his time to peruse her from head to foot he made her feel like her skin was electrified. She licked her lips, her mouth suddenly dry as she dropped her eyes away, taking in his leather jacket, the ripped jeans, and House of Rock t-shirt he wore.

He had 'bad boy' written all over him and for the first time in her life, Aubrey didn't think about her grades or her parents or doing the right thing. She let her heart and her body lead her.

"Now, what's a good girl like you doing at a party like this?" he asked his voice like butter on her senses.

She felt an intense desire to impress him, to show him she wasn't the good girl everyone thought. "How do you know I'm a good girl?" she asked, her sass seeming to surprise and delight him.

He raised an eyebrow and rubbed his thumb over his bottom lip as her eyes followed. "I would say the fact you're the only one not drinking the beer or the twenty-twenty," he said and grinned.

Aubrey wrinkled her nose as he named the popular alcopop.

He laughed again, a full-out belly laugh that made her toes curl in her trainers. "What's your name, bad girl?" he asked with a twitch of his lips.

"Brey," she answered not wanting to be Aubrey with him.

"Nice to meet you, Brey," he said as he took her hand in his and kissed the inside of her wrist making her feel things she hardly understood. "I'm Mickey but everyone calls me Knuckles."

"I'm going to call you Mickey because I'm not everyone," Aubrey replied having no idea where her confidence was coming from.

He tilted his head to the side and looked at her for a long minute, the intensity making her squirm. "No, you're not," he answered.

Aubrey spent hours that night talking to Mickey, they shared things nobody else knew about each other and at the end of the night as the party wound down, she shared her first kiss with the boy she knew in her heart she loved.

"Did you kiss him?" Madison asked as they cycled home.

"Yes," Aubrey blushed.

"Do you love him?"

"I don't know," she lied not ready to share these feelings with anyone else.

"Aubrey."

"What?" she snapped feeling irritated her sister was keeping on.

"Look."

Something about Madison's tone froze the blood in her veins. As she looked up at the still dark sky as they entered their street, she saw fire engines and police cars. Smoke and flames licked the night sky as terror clawed at her until she could hardly breathe. Dropping her bike, she ran towards her home that was engulfed in flames.

Strong arms caught her as she tried to fight her way free, her parents needed her. Everyone was looking at her and all she could hear was screaming, tears pouring down her face as the heat from the fire caressed her skin.

"No, no no no," she screamed, kicking out at the arms that held her immobile. Her eyes never leaving the burning house as she called for her mum and dad, all the while knowing in her heart that they were gone, and she would never see them again. That it was her fault this had happened. If she had been a good girl and stayed home instead of losing her heart to a bad boy, her parents would be alive, they would be with her. She felt her sister's arms around her, sobs racking her body as hers did and she held her tight. She watched silently as the fire was extinguished, the last swirls of smoke in the air, the smell would haunt her for the rest of her life.

She should have been here, she was a light sleeper and her parents were not. If she had been home, she could have saved them, but she hadn't been. Part of her wanted to blame her sister, to hit out at her for always making her follow her to protect her but as Madison looked at her with her heart as broken as hers, she knew she had to do what she had always done, she had to protect her baby sister.

So, as they drove away, and she saw the boy she had given her heart to sitting on his bike watching her with heartbreak and guilt in his eyes, she knew she had to turn her back on love and on bad boys. That way only led to pain.

CHAPTER 1

WILL WATCHED HIS FRIEND TAKE IN THE NEWS NOAH HAD JUST delivered and smiled. If anyone deserved it, then it was Nate. The guy was a natural father and loved Noah to distraction. He wondered if he would ever have kids. It wasn't something he had ever given much thought to, but as he did, his mind flew to Aubrey.

Her sweet smile, her beautiful dark brown eyes, the button nose, and the throaty laugh. She would be a great mum. He wondered again why she was hiding from him. Something kept telling him it was more than just him she was running from. He couldn't shake the fear that she was in trouble and needed him.

His fucking brother wasn't answering his calls since their fight, and he hated that their relationship was so fucked up because of the decisions he had made as a teenager. He knew he had cost Jack a lot, and he would carry that guilt forever, but he had tried to make it up to him without Jack knowing.

That was the thing about his older brother, he had to be in control just like their father. He was an uncompromising bastard too. He had no clue how his mother had put up with them all these years. But she had, and she did, even when she was sick from the chemo. She still stood by her husband and did all for him she could.

He remembered one Christmas when he and Jack were boys. He had worshipped his older brother, and Jack had been so patient and kind with him. He had been given a magician's kit, and Jack had got a Meccano set. Jack had been so excited, but instead of playing with his new toy, he had spent hours with Will playing magic. Will knew his brother hated it, but he did it for him. That was the kind of brother Jack was. Will missed him, the feeling like a fist to the gut, but he had nobody to blame but himself. It was why he had done what he had and why it was his closest guarded secret that only Zack knew.

His phone buzzed, and he took it out to check it. The name on the screen had his heart beating rapidly. "Dogberry?" he asked standing to leave the room.

"Boy scout," she replied.

"I take it this is not a Merry Christmas call especially as you called on a phone you shouldn't even know about."

"Oh, please, don't insult me, you don't honestly think I didn't know?"

"Yeah, good point. What can I do for you?"

"Your girl is in trouble and needs an extraction."

Will felt his heart beat double time as he locked eyes with Drew who was walking out of the dining room. "Where is she?" he demanded.

"In the middle of the Colombian jungle!" she said.

"Thanks, Dogberry."

"You owe me."

"Yeah, yeah whatever," he said hanging up.

Will looked at Drew and felt a plan forming. It was a lousy plan and would probably get him in a world of shit with his brother and Zack, but he had no choice—he had to help Aubrey. "Want to have some fun that will probably get us into a world of trouble?" he asked Drew who grinned slowly.

"Hell yeah, what's the plan?"

"We're going to steal a plane from Eidolon and fly to Colombia."

"Awesome. Who's flying it?"

At that moment Liam walked through the door, and they both turned and smiled at him.

"He is," Will said with a look of determination.

"Oh no, no fucking way. Jack would fucking kill me mate," Liam said backing up.

"Pussy," laughed Drew as Will raised an eyebrow.

"What did you say?" Liam asked with a tilt of his head which told Will that Drew had bated him into the job.

"You heard me," Drew laughed.

"I'll show you a pussy," Liam said with a sneer as he turned to go back in the dining room.

"Where the fuck are you going?" Will asked with a frown.

Liam turned around, his hands on his hips. "To finish my fucking dinner. That is good shit, and I haven't had a cooked meal in weeks."

Will grinned he guessed he could give him that for the shit they were all about to cop when his brother and boss found out what they had done.

"Fair point and that stuffing is amazing," Will said as they returned to the loud dining hall where everyone was now wearing cracker hats and chatting as they ate. He resumed his seat and grabbed the bowl of red cabbage, piling his plate high. It was the only veg he liked and with any luck, if he put enough on, Mimi wouldn't notice the lack of sprouts.

He looked up at Lucy's voice.

"Everything okay, Will?" she asked with a raised eyebrow.

"Yeah, just my mum on the phone," he lied as Luce raised her eyebrow again, her way of calling bullshit. He looked away and saw Zack looking at him with a frown. Sometimes it fucking sucked being surrounded by operatives. Getting anything past them was like getting a hooker into the Vatican.

"So, Celeste did you decide about getting Samson a girlfriend?" he asked knowing it would distract the attention away from him. Shovelling a mouthful of turkey and stuffing in his face he sighed. Liam was right, this was good and when he went after Aubrey, who knew when he would eat again.

"Yeah, we think we'll get him a friend, but probably a puppy as I think he will take to it better. Zin wants to train this one to work with him, so a puppy would be better," she said smiling at Zin.

"Oh, my God, a puppy!" Katarina exclaimed excitedly.

Zin smiled at his niece, the cold assassin was a complete pussycat with his family. Nobody would believe the difference Celeste had made to the man known to many as the Viper.

"You want to help us choose her?" he asked Katarina and Natalia as Roz glared daggers at him, and Kanan leaned back and smiled.

"Can we?" they asked K.

"Ask your mother," he replied with a wink to Roz.

Roz turned her glare on her husband then, and Kanan laughed and kissed her soundly. "Fine but don't even think of asking me for a puppy. I have enough to do, I don't need a puppy to run around after," she said to the girls she adored.

"And the metamorphous into a housewife is complete," Will said laughing, enjoying being with these people more than he ever thought possible.

This was his home now, and although he missed his mum, he did not miss the rigid control his father held over everyone. He wished his brother would tell him to fuck off and knew one day he would, and Jack would be happier for it.

"Don't you start teasing her," Mimi said with a stern face, "and where are your sprouts?" He saw Roz laugh and give him the finger discreetly. "Everyone has Brussels sprouts at Christmas. It's a tradition." Mimi continued as she stood and moved around the table to dish him up a spoonful.

"But I don't like them," he said with a look of distaste at the tiny green balls of putrid evil.

"I don't care, it's tradition and if my Nate can eat them, so can you. You need a healthier diet, my boy," she said as she kissed his head to ease the rebuke.

He had come to love Mimi as much as everyone else had. She was like a mum to them all, and he realised he missed that. "Fine, but I want extra pudding to make up for it," he said with a cheeky smile that generally got him his way.

"Eat up," she said with a nod and a wink.

Once he had finished his lunch and everyone was starting to disperse into smaller groups, he looked at Drew and Liam. Standing, he went to kiss Mimi and thank David, Reg, and Colin for such an excellent dinner and then slipped into Zack's office.

He wasn't surprised to see his boss sat at his desk waiting for him.

"Start talking, Will," Zack said without preamble.

Will moved to his laptop to check the scan he was running and saw it was complete. He could now download the programme he needed to hack the satellites in Colombia. "Nothing to say," he replied vaguely.

Zack stood abruptly. "Don't give me that shit. I'm not some fucking moron you can fuck with!" he barked.

"Fine, I got a possible location on Aubrey, and I'm going after her," he said ready for a fight, knowing how busy they were after landing a contract with the government to overhaul the security at significant terror target sites.

"Fine, make sure Lucy is up to speed and make sure you keep Drew out of trouble. He's your responsibility."

"How did you…" he started but stopped when Zack raised an eyebrow. "Okay, thanks," he said instead.

"Have you told Jack?"

Will felt his hackles rise at the question. "No and I won't. He had his chance to help me, and he didn't want to know, so now he doesn't get the chance to ride in like a hero."

"Come on, Will, it isn't like that, and you know it."

"Maybe, but all I know is I needed his help, and he said no, so I won't ask again. I'll do what I have to do on my own."

"And Liam?"

"We both know who pays Liam's wages and it isn't Jack," Will said hotly.

Zack nodded in understanding. "Fine, stay in touch and don't get killed." He walked to the door and stopped before turning. "Oh, and another thing, we never had this conversation," he said firmly and then left.

Collecting everything he would need, Will threw his bag on his back and moved to the back door where Liam and Drew were waiting for him.

"Well, me old mucker, what's the plan?"

"I don't really have a plan, except steal a plane from Eidolon and get to Colombia," Will responded as they walked to Drew's SUV.

"Good job I'm here then ain't it," Liam said with a cocky grin.

"Well, it isn't for your looks or dazzling company," laughed Drew as he started the vehicle.

Liam shot Drew the finger. "Fuck you. Women love me and if Jack fucks up my pretty face for helping you steal his toys, you're gonna owe me so big," he shot at Will as Drew laughed and pulled onto the road for the ten-minute drive to Eidolon.

"Fine, if my scary assed brother rearranges your face, I'll hire you to keep me safe from Mimi and her healthy diet," he said with cringe at the thought of her hiding his sweet stash.

"You should be fucking thanking her. That shit is bad for you," Drew flexed a muscle at Will, "if you want to have guns like this instead of those weedy things." He gestured to Will's arms, which while smaller than Drew's, were twice the size they were a few months ago.

"Yeah, yeah whatever, just drive douchebag." Will pointed at the road.

"Let's go get us some toys to play with," Liam said as Will looked out of the window and wondered if the woman he was falling in love with was safe and if she would appreciate his help or just tell him to fuck off like last time. The thought of either made him smile, he liked a snarky woman with spirit.

CHAPTER 2

As he strapped his seatbelt for take-off, Will thought about what had just happened and couldn't believe how easy it had been. They had literally walked into the Eidolon compound using Liam's codes, through the armoury where they had picked up some very nice and costly hardware along with some 'toys' that Liam assured him they would need, then loaded up the plane.

He knew the system would alert Jack that Liam had been inside the armoury and the locked warehouse where the vehicles were kept. He had set up the fool-proof system, so he knew how good it was. He could have circumvented the security, but something stopped him. Deep inside himself, he wondered if he wasn't pushing things with his brother. Jack finding out the secret Will kept would certainly bring things to a head, more than likely a bloody one.

The Learjet 35 they had borrowed from Eidolon only had the capacity to fly two thousand miles, so they would have to fly from the UK to Sierra Leone and then refuel and fly to Recife in the North West of Brazil before starting the final leg to Colombia.

Opening his laptop, he glanced at Drew who had pulled his beanie over his eyes and was now sleeping. That boy was either sleeping or eating, but he had quickly become one of Will's best friends. The time they had spent together as he helped Drew refine his abilities for coding and hacking had forged a friendship that Will now considered one of his closest. The fact that Drew hadn't asked any questions before following him and helping him out, even knowing the danger and the possible outcomes, cemented that bond.

That was another thing about Drew that most people didn't get. He was smart, more than smart, he was a fucking genius, but he hid it. Hiding behind the muscle and the banter as he fought his inner demons, placed there by a fucked-up father.

Will checked the downloads and was pleased to see they had finished installing. He could now position the satellites where he needed them. He also checked in and saw that Jack had received notification of Liam accessing the armoury. He wondered how long it would take before Liam had Jack on his ass once they landed.

He would not ask Liam to lie for him though, he and Jack had their issues, but he would not drag Liam any further into the shit than he already was. As it was, he would probably have to put his hand in his pocket for another Learjet.

Opening a new window, he started to follow the crumbs that Dogberry had given him and soon found a source who was willing to provide him with information on a woman matching Aubrey's description. Will arranged the meet, and then knowing he couldn't do anything else, closed the lid and his eyes.

He wasn't sure when she had gone from being a job to being his. But in between the flirting and the fun dates to throw her off the scent of the Fortis mission he had fallen for her. The love she had for her family, the dedication to her job, her values, her twinkling eyes, her mischief when she thought nobody was looking.

He didn't know how he would convince her to give what they had a go, because he knew she felt it too. But he had to try, he had never felt this way about a woman before. He'd had plenty of women in his bed, more than he could count and none that he remembered but Aubrey had never let him in her bed and she had made more of an impression than all the pussy in the world.

Nate had teased that it was because she was playing hard to get and maybe there was a certain element of that, but it was way more than that. He had a feeling that Aubrey had the ability to destroy him and that terrified him, but like the adrenalin junkie he was, it gave him a thrill too, and wasn't that just fucked up.

He needed some sleep, but when he did sleep it was to dream about Aubrey, her skin against his as she laughed and teased him about his ink obsession. Even in his dream, he saw the minute she had withdrawn from him. It was like a shield had come down and she had blocked him out, cutting him from her life with a coldness that did not reflect the warm, sensual, brave woman he had come to know. The woman who was so far under his skin, he still felt her touch even now.

"So now what?" Drew asked looking at Liam and Will with a sarcastic grin. They had arrived in Colombia after a long assed journey that nearly had them all arrested in Sierra Leone. Thanks to a very quick hack into the security at the airfield Will had learned the guard had a gambling habit. Having greased his palm with some cash, he had let them through.

"Now, my friend, we find us a place to stay. I for one am Kerry Packer," Liam said as he slung his bag into the boot of the SUV they had hired and got in the back.

"What the fuck does that even mean?" asked Drew as he slid in the driver's side and started the engine.

Liam shook his head in disgust. "You, my friend, need to brush up on your Cockney rhyming slang. It means knackered, Kerry Packer, get it?"

Will smirked and shook his head. "Nobody fucking gets it except you." He laughed as Liam shook his head again.

"Animals, you're all fucking animals," he said as he folded his arms and closed his eyes.

"Where to, boss man?" Drew asked as he looked at Will expectantly.

Will shrugged and opened his phone.

"Please tell me you have at least figured out a place for us to stay?" said Drew with glare now.

"I'll sort it now, don't be a dick," Will replied with a grin at his friend's glare. Using his phone, he hacked into the best hotel he could find and booked them a two-room suite under the same aliases as the passports they were using.

"There, all sorted. We're booked into the Hotel Cali Superb in Cali."

"And where the fuck is that?" Drew asked as he put the address into the GPS.

"Two hours from Buenaventura, which is where the last sighting of Aubrey was," he replied.

"Okay, makes sense, gives us some cover in the crowd."

"Exactly, and that's where my contact wants to meet us."

Drew threw him a look. "Could be a trap," he stated.

"It could, but until we get there, we won't know now will we." Will laughed at the look on Drew's face.

"No wonder they keep you locked away in the cave, you're nuts," Drew said with a grin.

Will laughed again. If it wasn't for the woman he cared about being in danger then he would be enjoying this little excursion.

"What do we have on Chopper and his merry band of psycho's?" Drew asked his tone serious.

"We know he's in Colombia and we have intel that he's working with Santiago Rojas. He's the largest exporter of cocaine from Colombia into the US. He rules this entire region from Cali all the way to the border."

"How does he export it? Do we know?"

"We think he's using canoes to get it into the ports unnoticed and onto container ships."

"Canoes? Are you fucking with me?" Drew asked his brow raised in suspicion.

"No, they canoe through the mangrove trees at night. The border guards that work that shift are paid off, and the drugs are smuggled on board."

"Fuck a duck and Chopper is working with them?"

"From what I can find out and what K and Zin's contacts tell us, yes. He's providing security and transport for the gun side of Rojas operation."

"And Winslow?" Drew asked his jaw hard at the mention of his father's long lost sister and leader of the Divine Watchers.

"No word on her yet but she was last seen in Brazil, and we know she has links to Chopper. It wouldn't surprise me to find her here seeking sanctuary with her ex-lover."

Drew didn't answer then, and Will let him have his silence. Finding out your aunt was the single biggest threat to the civilised world had fucked Drew good and proper. Only time and support from Kanan—of all people—had helped to start healing that wound.

Night was falling when they arrived at their hotel and checked in. Liam took the bags while he hacked into the hotel security and put the feed through his laptop. Entering their suite, Will walked straight towards the bedroom door, a hand-held bug detector in his hand as he checked the entire suite for bugs as Liam and Drew checked it for two legged threats.

Happy the site was clean he quickly put the feed from the hallway on an empty loop, so nobody could see if they were coming or going and used the technology he had developed for Zack and Eidolon to put a cone of silence around the entire suite. That way nobody could hear or see what went on inside.

"What time are we meeting the contact?" Liam asked.

"Twenty-one hundred hours in the hotel bar," he answered.

"And the contact is?" Liam asked.

"Her name is Siren. We haven't met, but I have assurances that she can be trusted."

"Assurances from who? You do know the meaning of the word Siren, right?" Liam asked with a grin.

"Fuck off, knob nugget. I got assurances from Roz."

Liam scoffed, and Drew groaned.

"Oh, great. We're dead. Roz would send us to our deaths just for shits and giggles," Liam said with a glare.

"Don't be a pussy, Liam. Roz is sweet when you get to know her," Drew defended.

Liam rolled his eyes and stood, moving to the fully stocked bar. "Just because she makes scones now does not mean she has become mother fucking Theresa. The woman is the deadliest assassin not known to man."

"I know that, but she is loyal, and I trust her and so should you."

Liam raised a glass of whisky to his mouth and downed it in one shot before answering. "Fine but when we're filleted and left for dead by this Siren don't say I didn't warn you."

"Whatever, just shut up you two and come and look at this latest satellite image from where we think Aubrey might have headed."

The two men must have heard the urgency in his voice because they rushed to him and peered over his shoulder.

"Oh fuck!" declared Liam with a groan.

"We're too late!" said Drew as Will felt his heart sink.

CHAPTER 3

Aubrey could just make out the man as he moved through the hot jungle towards the bar where her sister was. Bugs and all manner of creepy crawlies bit at her skin as she maintained her position, not wanting to look away in case something happened.

Her sister was young and hot-headed. She was going to get one or both of them killed if she kept on like this. Aubrey knew Madison wanted revenge for what Chopper had done to her, but to come here on her own to try and exact that revenge was fucking foolish at best, at worst, it was suicide.

She was going to get them both killed, apart from the fact that she was now suspended from her job thanks to it all. English had begged her not to go after her sister but how could she not? Ever since they were kids, she and Madison had been close, and she wasn't about to abandon her now. Moving as silently as she could, Aubrey eased towards the bar that was little more than a shack with all sorts of unsavoury men inside.

Drug lords, gun runners, guerrilla soldiers. These men had no morals, and her sister had taken a job at this dive bar to try and track down Chopper. She saw a man grab her sister over the bar, his sinister smile making her sick as he leered down at her sister's cleavage.

Bile crawled up her throat and not for the first time she wished she hadn't done this alone. She knew she could have asked for help from Fortis, but she was still fighting the ridiculous attraction to that tatted-up computer geek, who for some reason thought after one date and a kiss, he owned her body and could go around knocking her out. Just the memory of him doing that made her furious.

What a kiss though. She had spent many nights trying to forget it but found herself reliving it as her body heated with desire. The man was a menace. He was too sexy, too smart, and way too dangerous to her heart. Men like Will Granger had secrets, and they also didn't settle down. She had no intention of ending up as a notch on the sexy asshole's bedpost.

So here she was in the Colombian jungle trying to rescue her baby sister on her own with zero resources. She was so engrossed in the man that was now trying to kiss her sister that she never heard the man behind her. Not until it was too late, and a large hand slapped over her mouth, and a cloth bag was thrown over her head. Oh, how she wished she hadn't been such a wimp and had asked for Fortis' help.

They quickly and efficiently covered her mouth with duct tape and secured her wrists, while she fought them. She wasn't helpless and fought with everything she had, using every self-defence lesson she had ever learned through her police training and some she had picked up from Lucy and Emme when she had joined them for a few training sessions. Aubrey quickly realised that it would get her nowhere when she was subdued as if she was a child. She was hoisted over the shoulder of one of the men like a sack of potatoes.

Her cop instincts were on alert though and picking up as many details as she could as they trudged silently through the jungle. The first was that the men, and she guessed men, about four of them were trying not to hurt her. They also weren't speaking which told her these were not rookies, they were professionals.

She was carried for about five miles while the blood rushed to her head giving her a headache. She put up another token fight and got passed to another man for her trouble.

"Stop fucking around and stay still," he growled in a low, menacing and somewhat sexy voice, which if she wasn't mistaken was American. If he hadn't been her kidnapper, she could have happily listened to him all night. Suddenly they stopped, and she was put on her feet, the man who had held her steadied her before guiding her to sit in a vehicle.

"Step," he said as he guided her to step up into an SUV. Aubrey felt the others get in and the four doors close before the vehicle started up, and they began to move.

"Take off the bag," she heard from another man with a British accent. The bag was unceremoniously pulled from her head. Light filtered in and she blinked away the brightness focusing on the back of two heads—one blonde and one brown. Turning she looked at the heavily tattooed but seriously sexy man beside her who winked and grinned.

"Ma'am," he greeted her.

She scowled at his smirk and turned to look at the man to her left and gasped. "You!"

"Please hold the theatrics for when we see my brother, I have no use for it," said Jack Granger.

"Wow you really are an asshole, aren't you?" she asked with a raised eyebrow.

He looked her over with disinterest. "Apparently I am," he stated.

Aubrey watched as he answered a call. His answers were clipped and to the point just like the man himself.

"Why are you here?" she asked a few minutes later when his brief call ended. She thought Jack wasn't going to answer her as he looked through his phone reading something.

He looked up, and she was caught in the swirling brown depths of his eyes that held anger and annoyance. "To stop my brother from getting himself killed for a woman who doesn't give a shit about him."

"Will is here?" she asked as butterflies took flight in her tummy.

"Yes. He thinks he's going to rescue you, but he's more likely to get himself killed."

Aubrey felt outraged with the way Jack spoke about Will. "Hey, don't talk about him that way. He may not be all brawn and badass like you, but he is sweet and kind and so clever," she started and then stopped herself at the chuckle from the front of the car.

Her eyes caught those of the driver. "Will is very badass, and he's also extremely brawn now, honey. Our boy grew up and got himself some guns to go with his tatts."

"Well, it doesn't matter because Will and I are nothing to each other, we are friends at best."

"You defend all your friends like that?" Jack asked, and she went silent knowing her defence of Will had given her away. "Um," he said.

She bit her tongue from asking what that meant, but it came out anyway. "What does um mean asshole?"

"Maybe I was wrong about you."

"Yeah well, I was right about you. You are an asshole."

"Is that any way to talk to the man who just saved your ass from being raped and murdered?"

"I was fine. I was assessing the situation to decide the best way to get my sister out."

"Is that right? And don't tell me you let us sneak up on you because you knew we were there." He snorted with derision.

"Well, maybe not but I can handle myself with those guys."

"Get real, sweetheart, they would have caught you, and then you and your sister would be getting raped and sold," said the driver.

"Tone it down, Alex," said Mr Tattoo.

Alex threw him a glare in the rear-view mirror. "All I'm saying is you shouldn't be doing this alone."

"I'm not now am I, because you're going to help me," she demanded.

"No way!" Jack said coldly.

"Yes, way or I'm going to ask Will for help."

"Wow, you are a real bitch," Jack replied.

"No, but like you, I'll do anything to save my sister."

Aubrey watched as Jack looked out the window as they hit a dirt track that some would call a road and drove through what could be classed as a small village.

"Fine, but on one condition."

"Name it."

"Stay away from Will. He likes you, and despite our differences, I don't want to see him hurt."

"Done. I have no intention of hurting Will," she said with a knot in her belly because even though she had decided Will was too much of a risk for her heart, closing the door on a man like Will Granger was hard to do.

"Oh, and by the way," Jack started as he looked at her with annoyance, "your sister was picked up by Chopper's men just after we picked you up." His tone was dismissive as he looked away.

Aubrey said nothing, her pride wouldn't let her. She was however very thankful that she had secured their help, even at such a high cost. They drove the rest of the way in silence until they reached a small motel.

Mr Tattoo who had introduced himself as Reid cut the ties at her wrists before they stopped. "He isn't as big an asshole as he pretends," he said and grinned.

Aubrey raised her brow in surprise. "Yes, he is, but it isn't my problem. I just want Madison safe, so I can go back to my life and try and pretend this didn't happen."

"Fair enough."

Aubrey followed the men as they made their way towards the first floor. The motel was clean and small with bright green walls that almost made her vomit such was the contrast with the orange striped carpet.

"You can sleep in here. Blake will be outside the door, and we'll be next door if you want anything," Reid said as Jack and Alex disappeared through the door next to her.

"Thanks," she said and went to turn but stopped. "Reid," she called, and he stopped turning to look at her his piercing baby blue eyes assessing her.

"Yes?"

"Will, is he okay?" she asked wanting to hear that the man she couldn't stop thinking about was safe.

Reid smiled, and the action crinkled the corners of his eyes. "He is for now, but I'm not sure that will last when Jack gets hold of him," he chuckled.

"Oh, I see," she replied.

"Not sure you do, sweetheart, but okay. Holler if you need anything," he said, and with that, he left with a nod to Blake.

Aubrey moved inside and closed the door, flopping on the bed as exhaustion hit her. How did she get herself into this situation? Hot on the heels of that was thoughts of Will. He had come looking for her. If she was honest with herself, a part of her was doing somersaults that he cared enough, but the other part was terrified that she wouldn't be strong enough to walk away from him and honour the deal with Jack.

She had never met a man who could make her laugh, make her feel free and independent while still making her feel safe. Will had done all that, it was part of the reason she hadn't slept with him. His kisses made her knees weak, made her think of forever, and that was dangerous because men like Will didn't do forever, they did 'for now'. And once she slept with him and revealed her vulnerable side to him, walking away would be impossible.

Her last walk on the wild side had cost her parents their lives and she had no intention of taking another risk like that, and if it was one thing the computer genius was, it was wild. He was unpredictable and fun and did things without caring about the consequences, and it excited and terrified her. She was the safe sister—the sensible one—always had been always would be.

Madison was the wild one, and there was no room for two like her sister in one family. She and Jack had that in common, he was the sensible one too. Why couldn't she be attracted to him? But despite his gorgeous Henry Cavill looks, he left her cold. No, she wanted the man with the secrets, the man with stories on his skin that told of a history only he knew. She wanted Will, and she couldn't have him.

CHAPTER 4

"Are you sure about this?" Liam asked as they stepped off the elevator at 8:55pm.

"Don't be a pussy, Liam. If Roz trusts her, so do I," Will said as they walked towards the restaurant gathering the stares of more than a few women.

"Fine, it's your funeral." Liam shrugged as he winked at a maid that walked past him with an invitation in her eyes.

"You are such a dog." Drew laughed as Liam followed her swaying hips as she walked away.

"Shut up you two, we need to find this Siren and figure out what the fuck is happening," Will said exasperatedly.

He had felt the sick feeling in his gut ever since he'd seen the smoked out village close to the last sighting of Aubrey and Madison. If something had happened and he was too late, he would never forgive himself.

Moving into the bar, he felt someone's eyes on him and looked around but didn't see anyone. He went to the bar and ordered a beer as Drew and Liam took a seat close to the door. When he had asked Roz what Siren looked like, she had said not to worry as she would find him.

He had tried to search for any info on Siren and found nothing, which was what he'd expected. He was taking a sip of his beer, not really enjoying it, when he felt someone sit down beside him.

"I hear the Cider is good from your part of the world," purred a beautiful brunette with a slightly Cuban twang to her accent, although she tried to hide it.

"I hear your favourite movie is Bambi," he replied using the code Roz had given him.

"It is both sad and uplifting," she smiled, and her brown eyes twinkled.

She was stunningly beautiful, and Will could see how she had gotten her nickname. With long, jet black hair, warm olive skin, and sultry eyes that held more secrets than he could ever learn, Will realised that although she only hit five feet, four inches and barely fifty kilos or one hundred and ten pounds in the old scale, she was pure dynamite in an exquisite package.

"I hadn't thought of it that way," he said taking another sip of beer.

"I have a small amount of information on the woman you are looking for. But I need something in exchange."

"What is it?" he asked knowing that he would pay any price she asked.

"I need someone found."

"Surely Roz could help you," he said instead, wondering why she would come to him.

"She could, but I don't want her to know."

"So, you want me to find someone and keep it a secret from Roz?"

"Yes, and in exchange, I will help you find your woman."

Will considered it for a split second before answering. "Fine, but only after we find Aubrey," he said.

"Good, now tell your friends to join us at my table, and we will discuss what I know," she said as she smiled at him. Yep, that was why they called her Siren because when she smiled empires fell.

Will stood and followed her to a table in the corner with visual to the door and the windows without making them visible. He beckoned

Liam and Drew over as he scanned the room. He was getting a strange vibe from the hostess and the barman that had served him.

Liam and Drew sat down with their backs to the wall as did Siren leaving him with a clear line of sight to the door through the glass on the opposite wall.

"So, you're Siren," Drew said, and Will saw him appraise her, not like a woman although Will was sure there was a part of him that noticed her, but as a fellow operative.

"So the rumour goes," she replied taking a sip of her drink.

"Drew. Nice to meet you," he said with a grin as he reached out his hand to her which she took with only the tiniest of flinches that was barely discernible.

"What do you know of Aubrey?" Liam asked, the usually friendly man almost hostile towards Siren.

"She was seen on the outskirts of the Lost Village closest to Buenaventura."

"When?" Will asked.

"Last night," she replied as she crossed her legs, her tight black trousers skimming her ankles, the red stiletto heels looking more like a weapon than a fashion accessory.

"And now?" Will asked growing tired of the half answered questions when he sensed she knew more.

"Why don't you ask your friend here," Siren said, indicating Liam with a flick of her wrist. Will glanced at Liam, his jaw tight as anger and frustration gnawed at him. "Liam?" he asked his tone clipped.

Liam glared at Siren who just tipped her lips in a smile that would send men to their knees in prayer. Liam finally looked at him, and Will saw none of the friendly, happy-go-lucky man that Liam showed the outside world. He saw the man who had lost his best friend and still wasn't over it.

"Don't make me fucking ask again," Will ground out, his temper growing thin.

"Jack has her," Liam replied his eyes not leaving Will.

"Jack? My Jack?"

"Yes. He, Alex, Reid, and Blake found her in the jungle and took her to safety."

Will gripped the arm of the chair, fighting back the need to punch something. "What the fuck was he doing here in the first place and when did he get here? Did you tell him?"

"He got here last night, and no I did not fucking know he was here. Not until he called me earlier to ask why the fuck we stole his Lear jet."

"And?"

"And I told him I was helping a friend."

"What did he say?"

"He said I was fired and hoped I had fun. Don't worry, Jack fires me at least once a week," Liam said with little care that Jack had sacked his ass.

"Why was he here in the first place?" Will asked knowing that a showdown was coming between him and his brother and he now had a clue how things would stand afterwards.

"He didn't say. You'll have to take that up with him. Look, I should have said something, but I didn't exactly want to get caught in the middle of this family feud you have going on."

"Yeah, whatever. Don't sweat it. I'll take care of it, and if he does sack you, you can always get a job as a stuntman."

"Well, now that's out of the way, Drew, why don't you buy me another drink and tell me all about Roz and this husband of hers," Siren said to Drew.

"Of course," Drew said with a grin as he jumped up and walked to the bar with Siren behind him.

"Siren," Liam called, and she turned on her heel to look at him.

"Yes?" she asked, one perfectly arched brow raised in question.

"Don't mess around with the kid, he's been through enough," Liam said in warning.

Siren turned and looked at Drew as he stood at the bar, women flocking around him like flies to honey. "I think the kid can handle himself just fine." With that she sashayed away.

Will wondered at the look on Liam's face. "Where is Aubrey now?"

he asked wanting to see the woman who caused him to lose sleep more than he wanted his next breath.

"The team is getting a couple of hours rest, and then they're bringing her here."

"Fine, let me book some rooms." Will took out his phone and as he did it rang in his hand.

"Will?" the shaky voice asked.

"Yes, this is he."

"It is Pierre Aubin from the embassy."

"Hey, Pierre, good to hear from you."

"I wish the circumstances were happier. I need to meet you —alone."

"Okay, when?" Will asked, the hair on his neck standing on end.

"An hour. There is a bar near the East of Cali called *La Cantina*. Meet me in one hour."

Will looked at his dead phone and frowned, that part of Colombia was not exactly known for its big tourist welcome.

"Who was that?" Liam asked as he took a swig from the bottle of beer he had been nursing.

"Just a friend, nobody important," Will hedged, and so as not to tip Liam off, he finished his beer before standing. "I'm going to crash for a couple hours. What time do we think they will arrive?"

Liam tipped his head to the side silently assessing Will. "They should be here around zero five hundred hours. Look, Will, we cool? I should have told you about Jack."

"Nah, it's cool. We're good," Will answered and meant it. It wasn't his nature to hold a grudge, he left that to his brother. "Later," he said as he touched knuckles to Liam and left the bar.

As he stepped into the hallway, he saw Drew stepping into the elevator with Siren and grinned. That boy was quick, he sure would have his hands full with a woman like Siren though. Latina women were a handful in all the best ways. Drew might just have bitten off more than he could chew there. Moving to the stairs, he jogged to his room, needing the exercise to stop the angst in his blood from sending him crazy.

Slipping into his room, he scanned his laptop for any updates on a security breach on this floor and found none. Locating the Glock that Jack had given him a few years ago before he left for France, he slipped into the back waistband of his jeans and pulled his shirt over the top.

If he was going to meet Pierre in a dive bar in a dodgy part of town, he was going fully loaded. With a last glance around the room, he left to meet a very nervous friend. And hopefully, find out what the hell was going on before Aubrey got there and he had to split his energy between the upcoming fight he was going to have with Jack and persuading the woman he couldn't stop thinking about that he was worth a shot.

CHAPTER 5

USING THE STAIRS, WILL BYPASSED THE FRONT ENTRANCE AND ANY chance of running into Liam. He moved quickly down the street keeping his head down and away from the cameras pointed at the main road. Reaching the crossroads, he hailed a cab that immediately pulled across the line of traffic and made the other cars honk their horns in anger.

"A donde amigo?"

"Llevame a *La Cantina*."

"No no no amigo ese lugar es malo!"

"Sigue manejando por favor," Will said impatiently as he looked at his watch.

He saw the old driver shake his head and offer up a prayer. "Es tu funeral."

Yeah going to the Cantina probably is going to be my funeral!

"Yeah, yeah," he muttered low as he watched the bars and hotels give way to more modest homes. Then, as they drove further, he saw the signs of poverty creep into the barrios.

Homes became little more than shacks, and he wondered again what the hell was going on with Pierre. He had met the man when he'd done some work for Hunter McKenzie. Pierre was working at the French Embassy then and had been Louis'—who was Hunter's head of cybercrime—brother. Pierre had often come out on nights out with them before he had been transferred to Colombia during Will's last month in France.

Pierre was a nice guy, a little rigid sometimes but when he got a drink in him, he lightened up and was fun. Will had thought perhaps he had a thing for one of the IT test analysts that worked with Louis, but nothing had come of it, and the girl had gotten engaged last he'd heard.

The other burning question was why meet here? Pierre would stick out like a sore thumb in a place like this. At least his tattoos gave him some semblance of fitting in. Pierre was a sports coat and chinos guy and all but screamed money.

As the car bumped over the millionth pothole, Will ground his teeth to stop them from rattling loose. Eventually, the car stopped, and he leaned forward to thrust some cash at the driver. It was way more than the fare had been, but he knew the driver had taken a risk on him, and he wanted him to wait.

"I will give you another two-hundred pounds if you wait for me," Will said and prayed he said yes.

The driver looked around nervously, his eyes darting from one man to another on the dark street. "Thirty minutes, no more."

"Thank you," Will replied and exited the car.

He had rolled up his sleeves to show the array of tattoos on his forearms. He had learned a lot in juvie—the most important being that you needed to fake it and be the person they wanted you to be and never show fear. Showing fear was what got people killed more often than not in jail.

The bar looked like a cracked concrete slab with a small neon sign that said *La Cantina* above the door.

Stepping into the *La Cantina*, he glanced around at the long bar that ran from the front all the way down the left side. There were small wooden stools in front of it along the right side which was separated by only a metre at best from more stools and shelf where people could sit or stand there drinking.

The walls were covered in beer mats of every kind, the shelves behind the bar had glass that reflected the orange and yellow of the walls making it feel marginally bigger. Two men turned to look at him with suspicion written all over their faces. He was not welcome there, and he knew it.

Neither spoke as he walked to the bar and ordered a beer from the pretty young barmaid who was barely old enough to drink. Her face was full of make-up, her eyes filled with the tiredness and apathy of a much older person. She had accepted her lot in this life already, not even out of her teens and she was done with life. Her short skirt and midriff top barely covered her thin frame.

"Beer, please," he asked without making eye contact. Anything could set these men off, and if she belonged to one of them, he didn't want her getting into trouble because of him. He took the beer she gave him and laid the money down on the counter then moved towards the back wanting a clear view of the door. He watched as three men walked from out the back and noticed there was a rear exit that probably led into the alleyway that ran parallel to the road. The men gave him the once-over, doing nothing to hide the fact they were stacked to the eyeballs with weapons.

The men were barely out of their teens but already by his estimate they had tens of kills under their belts. It was the way of it here, the only way for them to make a life that wasn't leeched in poverty. But once they were in, there was no out, and they spent their usually short lives either killing or terrified that they would be killed. Most of these men would not be around long enough to see their babies grow up.

It was the sad truth in Colombia, the Cartels ruled here, and you either worked with them or starved. As he watched the men leave, he saw Pierre walk in. His friend looked so out of place as to be comical in any other situation, but here, he was literally taking his life in his hands.

Will nearly fell off his stool when the two men at the bar smiled and greeted him with warmth. Pierre seemed to have their respect, and that instantly put Will on edge. What could clean-cut Pierre possibly have that garnered so much respect from these dangerous men?

"Will," Pierre greeted with a relieved smile as he made his way to the back of the bar.

Will stood and greeted him with a handshake and a back slap. "Good to see you, man. How you been?" Will asked Pierre, looking at the enormous pupils of his friend's eyes and feeling his gut twist at the evidence of drug use.

"Good, good," Pierre said looking around nervously even though these men seemed to pose no threat to him.

Will had no idea what was going on, but he knew it was bad. "So, what can I do for you?" he asked as he watched another two men walk in the front door and make their way to the back. They made no pretence of giving him the once-over, making their suspicion of him evident. Will felt his neck bristle with tension. He shouldn't have come here, this had been a mistake.

He looked back to Pierre who was also watching the men as they retreated into the back door before glancing back at him and taking a swallow of the tequila that had been placed before him by the pretty young waitress. "Hey, Pierre," she said shyly, and Pierre grinned at her.

"Hi, Camila," he responded as Will watched the interaction with genuine interest.

There was something between these two, and they were trying to hide it. Will watched Camila walk away, and Pierre followed her every move with his eyes before turning to Will.

"I'm in trouble, and I need your help to get out of here," he said in a rush.

"What kind of trouble?"

"The kind that gets you dead if you say no," Pierre hedged.

"I need more than that," Will said casting his eyes around the room constantly, the feeling of being watched not unusual in a place like this, but this felt different, and he didn't know why. He watched Pierre look at Camila again, and his face softened telling Will more than his words ever would.

"Camila is Esteban Perez's niece. He's Santiago Rojas' second in command."

"And?" Will asked keeping his eye on the door as he heard gunfire in the distance.

"Camila is not like them, she's sweet and kind. We fell in love, and when Esteban found out I thought I was dead, but he said he was fine with it, that he would give his blessing if I started doing some small jobs for him at the embassy," Pierre said in a hushed tone.

"What's changed?" Will asked, instinct telling him something had.

"Camila is pregnant, and I don't want our child raised in this hell," Pierre said his voice laden with despair.

Will finished his beer and looked Pierre dead in the eye. "If I help you, will you promise to get clean?" He held up a hand before Pierre spoke. "And don't even think of lying to me."

"Yes, I will get help. Just please help me get her out of here. She will die here, and I can't bear that for her or our child."

"Fine, tomorrow night be ready, both of you. I'll contact you with the details at the embassy before noon." Will stood, and Pierre rose with him.

"Thank you, Will. You are a good man, and I won't forget this."

"Just be ready," Will said, then made his way to the door without a backwards glance.

Reaching the outside, he had to push past two men with semiautomatic weapons thrown over their shoulders like it was a fucking fashion accessory. Seeing the cab still there at the curb he almost sighed in relief.

"Thank you for waiting," he said, and the driver nodded and hit the gas before Will was even properly inside.

The driver just shook his head in the mirror and drove, and Will didn't relax until he saw the streets of Cali coming back into view.

Pierre had gotten himself involved with the head of security and second in command for one of the most feared drug lords in the world and definitely in Colombia. Santiago Rojas was an icon here and was feared and revered in equal measure.

What Will couldn't understand was why Camila was working in a dive like *La Cantina*. Her uncle was rich beyond measure in his own right, and surely his niece should not be working and living like she did.

He needed to do some research and find out more about the family dynamic and then find out what Pierre wasn't telling him because he had little doubt that Pierre had left out a shit tonne of information. But he was a good guy, and Will would help him out if he could. He needed to talk to Jack first though.

CHAPTER 6

Aubrey looked up at the luxury hotel as they pulled into the car park at the rear. She had managed to get a few hours rest, but in truth, she was tired to her bones still. A hot shower and some food had helped but worry for Madison had her playing over every bad scenario in her head, and with the predicament she was in, there were many.

Which only made her feel angry and then guilt for feeling anger that her sister had no thought for anyone but herself when she went and did the things she did, always relying on Aubrey to fix things. Madison had always been a free spirit and losing their parents at such an impressionable age had seemed to cement them in their childhood roles.

Aubrey knew she would forever feel responsible for her parent's deaths and looking out for Madison was something she would not fail at—no matter what. The guilt that plagued her only seemed to abate when a certain tattooed geek was around which was why she couldn't let him take what was left of her heart.

Just the thought of Will being so close made her feel giddy like a school girl. The flutters in her tummy, the excitement. What she wouldn't give to let that feeling have full reign, but she was here to get Madison to safety, and that was what she needed to concentrate on.

They exited the vehicles and Aubrey followed the men closely as they grabbed a bag each, and with Alex at her side and Blake and Reid following them, she stayed behind Jack as he walked to the reception desk.

The hotel was large and airy, with big potted plants, white marble floors, and high ceilings that gave the feeling of openness that she loved. Aubrey loved her surroundings to be open and large, light and inviting. The exact opposite of Will Granger with his dark clothes and his secrets.

"We have some rooms booked," Jack said to the man on reception who looked at them with curious eyes.

"Yes, you have rooms on the top floor," he said handing out cards and room numbers.

Jack turned and gave cards to Alex, Reid, and Blake before moving to the bank of elevators.

"Hey what about me?" she asked, her temper beginning to rise. Jack was a complicated man, to say the least, and she could totally see why he and Will got into fights. They were like chalk and cheese.

He turned to look at her over his shoulder, his sharp assessing gaze on her. "Here, it's the one next to Alex," he said handing her the keycard.

"Thank you," she said sharply as she went to take it, but Jack held onto it.

"Don't think about disappearing or next time I'll leave you to rot in the jungle," he said coldly.

God, why are the handsome ones such assholes? she thought as she rolled her eyes and yanked the keycard from him. "Don't worry, I won't be going anywhere until my sister is safe," she bit out.

"Fine," Jack said and nodded to Alex as he moved away from the elevators and towards the stairs.

She watched him go and wondered if he had been born with the stick up his ass or if the army had made him that way. "Was he born a jerk?" she asked nobody in particular as she stepped into the elevator with the other three men, who were no less intense than Jack but certainly more personable, well to her at least.

She heard Alex chuckle and looked up at the tall, gorgeous Cuban with golden blonde hair and warm, chocolate brown eyes. "Jack is a good guy when you get to know him and the best leader I have ever worked with, but when it comes to Will and anything to do with Will, he loses his head. Will and Jack have the ability to wind each other up with just a look."

"Yeah, well, it looks like you can add me to that list," she grumbled.

"Na, he just associates you with Will," Alex said and winked.

Good lord, that man was a walking sex dream, and yet he did nothing for her. Why, oh, why couldn't she fall for someone with fewer secrets, with less bad boy about him she wondered as the elevator stopped and Alex stepped out into the hallway, before allowing her to follow. This guarding her thing was getting old fast. She appreciated that they were looking out for her, but she was a trained police detective and not some little girl that couldn't look after herself.

She was about to gripe at Alex when she stopped dead at the sight in front of her. Her mouth dried up and her brain began to short circuit. She felt her heart begin to pound and her stomach buzzed with butterflies.

"Aubrey," Will said as he came towards her, wrapping her in his arms and holding her tight.

She didn't move for a second, and then as if her soul had seen the sun for the first time in months, she felt her body come alive. Lifting her arms, she wrapped them around his waist and held him, letting the comfort that only he could give her flow through her body.

The skin from his naked and very defined torso warmed her through her t-shirt, his body seemed alive under her hands. Her head rested on his chest, and she could hear the pounding of his heart. Aubrey felt safe and alive and home. It was only like this with Will, no other man had come close to making her feel this way—to breaking down her barriers, and yet with one look, one touch, and hers were crashing down around her.

The promise she had made to Jack to stay away seemed like an impossible task but one she had to fulfil, not just for her sister but for her own sanity. She let herself enjoy the feeling for one more moment before she gently pulled away.

Her eyes travelled over this new Will. He seemed so different to the cheeky gorgeous geek that so threatened her heart. This Will had ridges of muscle all over his flat, naked, tattooed stomach. Arms like bands of steel and pecs that would make a cover model drool with envy were devastating to her libido and her heart in a way that she knew if she didn't keep a distance, she wouldn't be able to remember all the reasons he was so dangerous.

"Are you okay?" he asked, and she dragged her eyes from his body to his face with the sparkling eyes and the grin that never seemed far away on his lips.

"Maybe you should put some clothes on before we talk," she said, and he smirked knowing precisely what he was doing to her.

"Yeah, man, cover that shit up in public." Blake laughed as he walked past Will towards his room, exchanging a fist bump with him first.

"You're just jealous, because you're getting flabby." Will laughed as Blake shot him the finger and closed the door.

"New tatts man?" Reid asked looking at the Angel wings tattoo Will had on the left side of his neck.

"Yeah," Will said rubbing the intricate tattoo with his fingers. Aubrey followed the movement studying the tattoo and wondering what it meant.

"Nick do it?" Reid asked as he walked to the room farthest down the hall.

"Yeah, nobody else gets to ink this skin," Will replied.

Reid saluted him. "True dat," he said with a smile before opening the door and stepping in.

"Aubrey, your room is next to mine," Alex said as he turned to leave.

Aubrey watched Alex go to keep her eyes off the sexy man in front of her.

"Can we talk?" Will asked, touching her arm gently with the tips of his fingers.

She followed the movement fighting the electricity she felt from his touch. "I'm not sure that's a good idea," she started.

"Please, Aubrey. I don't know what I did to upset you but let me fix it, please?" he asked, and she knew her resolve was weakening.

"Okay but put a shirt on first then come over. I'm in room eight," she answered and saw the grin spread across his face. *Shit, how do I arm myself against that?*

Letting herself into her room, she realised Will was in the room opposite. Dumping the small bag of essentials Jack had allowed her to pick up on their way over on the sofa, she looked around the room. It was plush, with thick cream carpets throughout, long, draped silk curtains in light champagne hung at the large windows to the balcony. A bedroom to the left held a large king-sized bed with navy blue satin sheets and large lush pillows. To the left of that was a huge bathroom with a jacuzzi tub and separate shower.

She looked longingly at the tub, desperate to soak her tired body in hot scented water for a few hours but knew she didn't have time. It was already midnight, and she needed sleep. But first, she would let Will say his piece before she settled things between them. Wanting to shower away the dust and grime, she quickly shed her clothes and turning on the hot water, jumped under the spray.

Hot water hit her skin like prickles, washing away the dust and exhaustion. Filling her hand with shampoo provided by the hotel, she massaged it through her hair and scalp. Swiftly rinsing off and stepping out, she wrapped a towel around her body and head.

Feeling much better equipped to handle Will now she was clean, Aubrey towelled off and stepped into sleep shorts and a vest. It was no more revealing than shorts and a t-shirt, so she had no worries that she was leading Will on. Leaving her hair to dry naturally, she was pouring herself a stiff drink of whisky when the knock came.

Drink in hand she moved to the door and checked the peephole. Seeing Will's tall frame, she unlocked the door and let him in. He stepped past her and his scent filled her nose, the sexy citrus smelling shower gel he used almost making her groan with a need for him to touch her. "Would you like a drink?" she asked.

"Na, I'm good," he replied looking unsure of himself.

Aubrey slung back her drink and moved to pour herself another knowing she would need it for the subsequent conversation. She felt him before she saw him as he walked up behind her, her skin hyper-aware of his every move. He didn't touch her though, merely stayed close, silently invading her space and her soul.

"I missed you," he said honestly, and it wasn't what she had expected, and the one thing guaranteed to bring her defences low. She had expected him to berate her for ignoring him, to yell at her for being reckless with her job and her life but the brutal honesty had her stopping short.

Turning, she found herself caged in his arms against the bar. His lips were so close, the lines of the images on his skin seemed to ripple with life. His blue/grey eyes were so full of emotion—an emotion she couldn't pin down, but she saw frenzied desperation in them.

"I missed you too," she found herself admitting.

"What happened? What did I do?" he asked as he stroked a curl back from her cheek, the contact making her shiver.

His lips were so close, and the air around them was charged with electricity that was making her body tingle with need for him. She and Will had kissed before, but this felt new, it felt different, as if every cell in her body was screaming for him and he hadn't even kissed her.

Her head was fighting for her to stay strong to stay away from his brand of sex, from the almost drug-like effect he had on her. One that could cost her every ounce of peace she had, but her body wasn't listening, and her heart had already given up the fight.

CHAPTER 7

"You didn't do anything. It's what you could do if I let you in that made me run." Her honesty shocked her, let alone Will. She watched as the intensity left his handsome face and a crooked smile appeared.

"You like me, you like me a lot," he said with a smugness that almost made her laugh as she pushed past him, ignoring the burn through her thin vest top as his hand skimmed her tummy as she did.

"I find you marginally less irritating than most men. That is not an admission of love," she said sucking in a breath now that she had some space between them.

He shook his head, and his hair flopped over his forehead adorably, making her want to brush it back with her fingers. "Uh, uh no way. You're not backing out of this now. You like me, and it scares you to death," he said, his voice suddenly becoming serious again. "It scares me too, Aubrey. I've never wanted to be in a relationship, but when I look at you, I can't see anyone else in my future. What terrifies me more is not finding out if this could be something special," he finished as he looked at her with nothing but sincerity in his voice.

"But what if being with you costs me everything else?" she asked with a wobble in her voice.

He moved to her then and sat on the end of the couch, pulling her between his braced legs. She went willingly not able to resist the pull between them. "What if not being with me costs us the greatest gift we have ever been offered?" he countered as he played with the tips of her fingers, before linking them and bringing them to his heart.

"I don't know if I can do it," she said on a rush.

She saw the desire in his eyes, the need for her to say yes and all she wanted to do was fall into him and tell him she could do it. But then her vision filled with the fire that had burned her home and took away her parents and all because she had fallen for a bad boy who so reminded her of Will.

"How about we go slow and take it from there?" he asked with a tilt of his head and a grin that made her melt.

His suggestion confused her though because she had thought that was all she wanted—to be friends, be in the safe zone but Will saying it made her feel like a lead ball had settled in her gut. What a mess she was. She had no idea what she wanted, or maybe she did, and she was just too chicken shit to go after it. "Okay. Friends for now and see what happens," she agreed with a nod.

Will kissed her palm before releasing her hand, and she felt the loss of him immediately. "Of course, if you want that to be friends with benefits, you only have to say the word, and I'll have you screaming for my cock before you can finish the sentence." He winked to show he was joking but it was too late, the image was already in her brain and it made her body burn.

Will smirked as he looked at her vest top and saw that her nipples were practically waving an invitation at him.

She crossed her arms to hide her treacherous body's response to his words and scowled. "Uncouth jerk," she hissed with as much heat as she could muster.

He strolled to the door and then turned back to look at her. "That's why you love me." He winked and then left with a quiet snick of the door.

That was the problem, she had an awful feeling that she was

already in love with him and she didn't know if she could stop it or even if she wanted to.

~

WILL HAD a grin on his face as he left Aubrey in her room. The relief at seeing her had quickly given way to the desperate need to touch her. But he was no fool and knew if he pushed too fast on this she would bolt.

Despite her outer confidence and appearance of being so put together, Aubrey was fragile in a way that didn't allow for her to relax. She took on too much responsibility, and her sister needed a kick in the ass.

He had agreed to go slow because he knew it was the only way to keep her close without scaring her away. Hearing that she was terrified of him had been a shock but in a good way because it showed the depth of her feelings were the same as his.

Seeing her had cemented in his mind how much she meant to him and he hadn't been lying when he said the thought of not finding out what they could have together scared him to death.

He had watched his teammates find love—Zack, Dane, Lucy, even Daniel and he wanted that for himself. He was sick of being alone. Of atoning for something that had happened when he was barely an adult and not able to make the right choices. He deserved to see if Aubrey was his soul mate and he would do whatever it took to find out.

It was time for the secrets of the past to make way for the healing of the future, and if that meant old hurts were aired, and relationships changed for better or worse, then he would have to face that, because he would not live in the dark any longer. It was time for the past to be laid to rest.

With that thought in mind, he made his way to the room he knew his brother was using and knocked. He had seen Jack come in when the cameras in the hall had picked him up.

He listened as Jack moved to the door and undid the locks before swinging it open and glaring at him. Before Jack could come up with a sarcastic opening Will raised his fist and punched him in the face.

CHAPTER 8

JACK STAGGERED FOR BARELY A SECOND AS WILL PUSHED INSIDE AND slammed the door closed. Jack rushed at Will, and he braced as Jack, who was stronger and so much more trained in hand to hand, hit him in the solar plexus with a jab. He felt the air leave his lungs in a whoosh as he staggered and tried to breathe.

"You hit like a girl," Will said as he slumped in the closest chair to catch his breath.

"Yeah well, at least I don't look like one with all that flowery shit on my body. You're a real prick, you know that?" Jack said as he wiped the smear of blood from his cut lip.

Will smiled in satisfaction at that. "Yeah, yeah so you keep telling me. Why are you here, Jack?" he asked with sudden exhaustion.

Jack looked him over as if studying a bug and finding it was poison. "To save your sorry ass from being killed when you went after a woman who doesn't even want you."

Will felt the hurt of his older brother's words pierce him deeply, causing the festering scab that was their relationship to bleed even more. "Wow. I bet that felt good," Will responded.

"Are you fucking kidding me? Do you think I want this shit all the time? I'm probably going to lose my job over you again. Again, you've ruined my life, and still, I run out to save your sorry ass."

"You're not going to lose your job," Will said as he stood and moved to the bar.

"What the fuck do you know, you tosspot? Why don't you go back to hacking shit and leave the real work to the men," Jack snarled as he paced, running his hands through his hair.

"That's the thing, Jack, you've never seen me as a man. All you see is the kid who fucked up, and you're never going to get past that no matter how hard I try."

"This is you trying?" he snorted with derision.

"I've done nothing but try since I got out of juvie. I keep trying to make amends to fix what I did wrong, and you just don't want to know. It's so much easier to blame me than to look too hard in the mirror and see your own failings."

"Me? What the fuck did I do?"

"You fucking left me with him, with our sad fucking excuse for a father. Went off and joined the army and forgot me."

"Is that what this is about? Me leaving you? Grow up, Will. People leave, they find jobs. It doesn't mean those left behind go and hack a fucking bank to get some attention."

Will crossed to the window and opened the balcony doors letting the air cool his skin and soothe his temper. "You'll never see the truth, so if you want me out of your life, then I'm gone," he said as he turned to Jack.

"Argh," Jack boomed and punched the wall beside the balcony door leaving a hole in the plaster. He glared at Will with fury and something else—guilt. "You're driving me fucking nuts. I didn't say that. I just want you not to fuck with my career. Don't break the fucking law or steal planes from the company I work for. Have you any idea what will happen when my boss finds out? He's going to fire me. He trusts me to run Eidolon with integrity and efficiency, not run across the other side of the world to rescue my baby brother's girlfriend. You know what, I should quit. It would be for the best. That way I might be able to get another job—maybe."

Will watched Jack pull out his mobile phone and dial the number he knew by heart and held his breath. It was now or never—the time was coming. Jack held the phone to his ear, and in his pocket, Will's phone began to ring. As if in slow motion, Jack turned and locked eyes with Will.

Will didn't back down or move a muscle as Jack, his older brother and the man he had looked up to his entire life, seemed to take in a hundred different things at once.

"Give me your phone!" he stated with a deadly calm that would have many an opponent shaking in their boots. With a calm he didn't feel inside, Will withdrew his phone and handed it to his brother knowing what he would see.

Jack held his eyes for a second longer before they dropped to the phone in his hand and that was when he lost it. "Motherfucker," he bellowed as he dropped both phones to the ground and grabbed Will by the collar before shoving him against the glass railing of the balcony. Will didn't fight back but held his hands up in supplication.

"All this fucking time and I've been answering to you, kowtowing to you after it was you who cost me my career in the armed forces."

"It isn't like that," Will said as his heart thudded in his chest.

Jack shoved him away and looked at him with real hatred. "Save it, whatever you say will probably be bullshit anyway. At least this way I can quit in person. Consider this my resignation. I'll get Madison back for Aubrey, and then I'm gone."

Jack stormed off and Will knew to go after him was the wrong move even though he desperately wanted to. Walking to the bar as he heard the door to the room slam shut, he poured himself a healthy slug of whisky and necked it back, feeling the burn all the way down his gullet.

He had hoped that when it eventually came out, it would be in a controlled setting, but there was nothing for it now. Jack now knew that Will was the owner of Eidolon—he just needed to persuade his brother to keep on running it because despite their differences, he didn't want anyone else.

Placing the glass on the side of the bar, Will walked to the door and opened it to find Aubrey poking her head out. Her eyes moved to him, and she frowned. *God, she's beautiful in those tiny shorts and top.* But he thought she could have made a sack look like a designer gown. With her looks and figure, she could have easily been a model, but her sharp brain and fight for justice saw her become a police detective.

She was bloody good at it too. He hoped to see her return to her career when this settled, and he would pull any strings he could to see that happen.

"Is everything okay?" she asked as he moved towards her, his hands in his pockets to stop himself from reaching out and touching her.

He stopped when he was a foot from her not trusting himself to go closer unless she invited it. He needed her to take this next step. "Jack just got some news he wasn't expecting, plus I punched him in the face." He shrugged.

"Will!" she exclaimed as she crossed her arms.

All at once five doors opened and Blake, Alex, Reid, Liam, and Drew moved towards them.

"Are you fucking serious?"

"You're the boss?"

"This is bloody priceless." Blake, Alex, and Liam spoke at the same time as the four badasses converged on them.

"I guess you heard then?" Will asked with a smirk.

"I can't believe you're the man behind Eidolon. All this fucking time we've been racking our brains, trying to figure it out and it was you," Alex said.

"Why did you hide it?" Drew asked with his head tilted. His hair was a mess as if he had been in bed for some time.

Will shrugged. "I didn't do it for glory, I did it because my brother needed it and I had the funds to make it happen."

"But why not tell him?" Reid asked as he rubbed his chin.

"Because Jack would never have accepted it. Am I right?" said Aubrey.

Will turned to her and smiled. She got it, she understood why he did what he did. "Exactly. Jack would see charity and wouldn't have done it. All he sees is the fuck-up who ruined his life. This way he got to do what he loves, I got to feel less of an asshole, and hundreds of people have been saved by the work we do."

"But why not work for Eidolon? Why work for Fortis?" Liam asked.

"I don't want to run a business. I don't want to work with Jack, and I love Fortis and what we do there. Zack is the best, and I love the team like family without having the shitty history. Except for you, Drew. You get on my nerves," he joked at Drew who shot him the middle finger.

"Dickhead," Drew replied.

"Plus, I do all the IT work for Eidolon anyway and contract out to you guys anytime you need me too."

"Well, as much as I would love to stand out here all night and discuss the family dynamic between you all I'm knackered, so if you don't mind, I'm off to bed," said Aubrey.

"Yeah, I guess we should go and see if the boss has calmed down," said Reid.

"Yeah, wait up, I'll come too," said Drew as the four men headed for the elevators.

He watched them go and then turned to Aubrey who was watching him.

"You did a good, Will. I'm starting to think there's more of a good boy under those tattoos than a bad one." She laughed then at the thought.

"Why don't you let me in and I can show you how good I am?" he said with a leer and laughed.

"You can sleep beside me if you want, but only sleep," she warned with a finger in his chest as he moved her back into the room.

"Scouts honour," he said with a salute.

"You were not a scout." She laughed again as she walked back towards the bedroom.

"I sure was. I was in the Eleventh Hereford Scout group," he said as she tilted her head and he fought the groan as she bit her bottom lip.

"Well, in that case, I know my virtue is safe," she said as she crawled up the bed and under the covers, giving him the perfect view of her sexy curvy ass in those shorts.

With an audible moan, he turned his back and taking off his jacket threw it on the chair in the corner of the room. Sitting down he shucked his boots and then stretched out next to her on top of the covers. He wasn't a saint after all.

Lifting his arm, he invited her to cuddle up to his side which she did without hesitation. Aubrey rested her cheek on his chest, and he cursed the material that separated her silky skin from his. Draping his arm over her shoulder, he used the other to flick off the light.

"Thank you, Will," she said so quietly he almost didn't her.

"What for, beautiful?"

"For coming for me, even though I was a bitch."

"You were not a bitch, and I'll always come for you, Aubrey. The quicker you start believing that, the quicker we can get to the good stuff," he said as he traced the skin of her arm with his fingertips.

"I'm so worried about Madison," she admitted showing a chink in her armour.

"I know, but the guys will get her back and if there is one thing I know about the Herbert women—it's that they are strong and resilient. She'll keep herself safe until we can get her out."

"What if they hurt her?" she asked, and he knew very well what she was asking.

"Then we deal with it. There's nothing else to do except move forward and play the hand you have."

"I guess I've spent so long looking out for her it's hard to let go. I keep wanting to fix it all for her."

He could hear the exhaustion and worry in her voice now, and he wanted to strangle Madison for putting her sister through this. Instead, he said, "Get some sleep, you must be exhausted." Within minutes she was snoring softly in his arms.

Will lay awake thinking about what had happened with Jack and trying to figure out if he could have handled things better. The result was always the same, Jack would have reacted badly whatever he did. Once his brain was done with that, he knew he had to figure out how to get Camila and Pierre to safety by noon tomorrow and then there was Madison who was still with Chopper.

What a fucking mess he was in, but right now with Aubrey in his arms, he didn't want to think about that. There would be time enough to talk to Jack or Alex about Madison, and he would reach out to Zin first thing about helping Pierre and Camila.

Now he just wanted to enjoy the feel of the warm woman who was curled in his arms.

CHAPTER 9

The bar was almost empty as Jack tossed back his third glass of eighteen-year-old whisky like it was water. His brother was paying so he didn't give a fuck if he drank it like it was cheap shit. He lifted his hand and shook the glass at the bartender who was polishing glasses at the other end, indicating he wanted a refill.

The bomb his brother had just dropped was still reverberating around his brain. How had he not seen it? How had he been working for his brother this entire time and not known who was behind Eidolon?

He had come to think of it as his. He had free rein on all missions and jobs he took, he had complete autonomy over what to buy, who to employ—for all intents and purposes it was his company, and he ran it as such.

It all made sense now, how he was approached and when. It had all seemed so fortuitous coming on the back of what had happened with Will. When Will had hacked the bank and moved around those funds, it had wrecked his family. His mum had almost had a breakdown, his dad had disappeared for months on end, taking on more extended deployments in Afghanistan and his career in the SAS had been cut short in its prime.

But Will had never seemed to understand what he had done. Jack knew in his heart that Will hadn't meant to hurt anyone, that his brother was not a bad person, but his selfish act had cost everyone—most of all Will himself. Watching his baby brother—the brother who he had adored—being locked up with his whole future in jeopardy had almost killed him.

That was what made Jack so angry. Will was gifted beyond what anyone could comprehend. The systems he had designed had made him millions of pounds before he'd even reached nineteen. He had saved more lives with the programmes he had written and the information he had found than even he could understand. Will was good to his core which was why Jack couldn't understand why Will had never come to him.

Jack had no doubt in his mind that Will had hacked that bank for someone else, he would never have done it otherwise. Not his sweet baby brother who had crawled in his bed in the middle of the night when the monsters scared him. Not the boy who had cried when a frog had gotten trapped in their car and died from the heat, not the boy who had followed him around imitating everything he did.

Will had accused him of turning his back on him, but it had been Will who had changed, who had locked him out of his world long before he left to go in the forces. What he didn't know was why, and to this day he didn't know, even though he had tried to investigate and find out his reasons. In the end, he had taken his father's advice and given up. His old man was a tool, but in this instance he was right. If Will wanted to keep secrets, then he'd had to accept that but to now find out that after all this time his brother was, in fact, his boss, grated like an open sore rubbed with salt.

The hypocrisy did not sit well with him, and he was done trying to figure it all out. If Will wanted to play games, he could play them on his own because he was done with it all. He could go contracting, fuck, he could probably go and get a job working for Zack.

Looking into the glass behind the bar as he slugged back the fourth whisky, Jack tried to suppress a groan when he saw Liam, Alex, Drew, Reid, and Blake walking towards him. Just what he fucking needed, a pep talk from this lot. He knew that look on Alex's face. That was his 'let's fix this and all be friends' look.

The Cuban with model looks was as deadly as they came. He could take out a cartel single-handed and had when he had worked undercover, but he was also the fixer of the team. If something was going wrong, it was Alex who fixed it. If someone was hurting, then Alex would fix it.

He was also the one-night-stand king. Women dropped their underwear for him at the slightest encouragement, and he never called them back and yet on the rare occasion he ran into one of those women, they still wanted more. Although that had been dubbed the Eidolon effect because none of them had any trouble getting laid.

"Don't want to hear it!" he stated as they reached him, and Blake and Alex sat either side of him.

Alex just looked at him and motioned the bartender. "Five more of whatever he's drinking," he asked, and Jack felt his eyes on him.

"Did you not hear me?" Jack asked caustically.

"We're as shocked as you, Jack, but don't throw the baby out with the bathwater, mate," Liam said as the drinks were lined up in front of them.

"You're still fired, Liam," Jack bit out.

"Yeah, yeah, whatever," Liam replied.

"I honestly don't see what the big deal is," Drew said, and Jack turned to glare at him.

"Who the fuck asked you anyway? You're Fortis, this is an Eidolon meeting so get lost."

"Ignore him, Drew. Jack is being a bit of prick right now and doesn't know what he's saying," Alex said as he sipped his whisky.

"The fuck I don't," replied Jack slamming his glass down. "I'm still in charge of this shit storm, and you assholes, so mind what the fuck you say to me," Jack yelled as he got up and the room began to spin. He shot out a hand to grab the bar and Blake steadied him. "I'm fine," he slurred as he righted himself.

"Go to bed, Jack, you're no good to anyone like this and we still have to sort out a plan to rescue Madison."

"Yeah, it's all her fault, her and that sister. If it weren't for them, this wouldn't have happened, and my life would not be in the shitter," he slurred as he swayed towards the exit.

Alex caught up with him. "You can't blame Aubrey. She was just doing exactly what you would have done if it were Will."

"Yeah and look where that got me. She should cut all ties and lead her own life. Let her sister fight her own battles."

"Yeah okay, Jack." Alex helped Jack into the elevator. "Can you get back to your room okay?" Alex asked.

"Fuck off, Alex," he said as the door began to close and the room spun. He didn't need anyone feeling sorry for him, and he didn't need their help. He was going to be a lone wolf from now on he thought as he pressed the button for the top floor. The elevator lurched, and Jack grabbed for the rail along the middle. For a moment, he thought something had happened then realised he had reached his floor as the doors opened, and he stumbled towards his room.

He stopped, and for a second, he was tempted to give Will a piece of his mind—to tell him how his secrets had fucked their family up but the tiny part of him that wasn't drunk decided to wait until he had a clearer head.

Opening the door, he shut it quietly and then fell onto his bed with his clothes on. He was exhausted from always being in charge, of going from one job to the next and never letting his guard down because when you did that, that was when shit went wrong.

Maybe he would take a holiday after this was all over was his last thought as he fell into a booze-induced sleep.

∼

ALEX WATCHED his boss as he hit the button for the top floor and shook his head. This had been coming for a while. The tension between Jack and Will had been building for months. He just hadn't expected this to happen. Will as the leader of Eidolon—*shit* that was out of left field.

He thrust his hands in his pockets and winked at the sexy brunette on reception who had been flirting with him earlier. She reminded him of Evelyn, his sweet, innocent Evelyn—the girl who had stolen his heart when they were barely teenagers and had crushed it when she had disappeared.

He wasn't sure if he would ever stop looking for her in the eyes of every woman he met. Even at seventeen, he had known she was his soul mate, the other half of himself and he was sure she had felt the same. Just as they had been getting ready to run away together to escape their families and all the preconceived ideas they had—she had disappeared leaving him distraught.

Deciding he needed a drink more than he needed to get laid, he moved back into the all-night bar and saw Drew was the only one at the bar now. "You can't sleep either?" he asked as he climbed onto the stool beside Drew.

Drew looked at him with a shrug. "Na, I'm too wired to sleep," he said as he sipped a beer.

"Yeah, lots of shit coming out of the woodwork tonight," Alex said ordering a beer too.

"Jack is intense, isn't he?" Drew said.

"He can be, but he's a great leader and a good friend. Nobody I would rather have in my corner than him. He would die for those he cares about and despite the way they are, Will is top of that list."

"Families are fucked up," Drew said with a small laugh. "I should know, most of mine are batshit crazy. Except for Lauren and the twins. I would die for them in a heartbeat."

"Yeah, I get that, I think everyone has their secrets."

"Yeah, I guess we all do," Drew said.

"So, tell me about Siren. Liam says she's one of Zenobi's. I haven't met her, but he says she's beautiful."

"Yeah, she is stunningly beautiful, and she has that sexy Latina vibe going on."

"Be careful with that one then, Drew, because Latino women have a habit of getting under your skin and settling themselves in your heart like no other women on earth."

"Sounds like there's a story there," Drew said with a smirk.

Again, Evelyn's image came to him, her long dark hair blowing all around her face in the evening breeze as they sat by the river and talked about all their hopes and dreams for the future. "Let's just say when you give your heart to one, they don't ever give it back. Even if it's crushed into a messy, bloody pulp, they hang on to it until all you have left is memories," he said revealing more than he ever had before.

"I'm sorry," Drew said looking at him with sincerity.

"Shit happens, just be careful."

"Don't worry, Siren and I are just friends, the flirting is fun and if it leads to some no-strings sex then all good, but for now, I just want to concentrate on finding my aunt and stopping her for good. My heart isn't involved at all."

Alex nodded and knew that Drew had struggled with finding out Rhea Winslow, the evil leader of the Divine Watchers, was his aunt. Fuck who wouldn't fight with that?

"A toast," Alex said raising his glass, "to fucked up families and no-strings monkey sex," he said as Drew laughed and knocked their beers together.

"Amen," laughed Drew.

"Now, I should probably try and get a few hours' sleep as we have to find Madison tomorrow. I don't like the idea of her with Chopper." Alex frowned at the thought.

"We have any leads?" Drew asked as he finished his beer and stood, to walk to the elevator with him.

"Not anything new, but Decker is working on something with Mitch at the moment."

"Does Zack know?"

"Yes, all info is being shared between Fortis, Eidolon, and Zenobi."

"Isn't that unusual?" Drew asked as they stepped off the elevator onto their floor.

"Yes, but so is the threat."

"I guess I still have a lot to learn," Drew said

Alex chuckled. "You'll get there. It takes years and years of experience to get to where Zack and Dane are, but you have good teachers. I mean, they aren't as good as Eidolon, but Fortis is okay," he teased as Drew laughed and disappeared into his room.

That kid had an old head on young shoulders, he wasn't sure if he had been as canny at twenty-three. Locking his door, he checked for emails before stretching out on the bed and falling into a fitful sleep filled with eyes of melting chocolate and skin like warm honey.

CHAPTER 10

The beeping of the alert on his watch telling him there was a breach on their floor woke him seconds before the door to Aubrey's room came crashing in. Will jumped from the bed as Aubrey reached for her bedside drawer. Pressing the button on his watch that was linked to Liam and Drew, he put himself between Aubrey and the bedroom door as he heard shouting.

The door was thrown open, and Will found himself face to face with four armed police officers and they all had their weapons trained on him.

"What the hell is going on?" he demanded as he glared at the short, uniformed policeman that seemed to be in charge.

"Will Granger, you are under arrest for the murder of Pierre Aubin," he said with a sneer as two of the armed men stepped forward and hauled him across the bed, shoving his hands behind his back and cuffing him.

"What the fuck! I didn't kill anyone," he said as he began to struggle. The policeman hit him with a baton, and he felt his knees give as pain lashed through his head.

"Where are you taking him?" yelled Aubrey as she glared at the policeman who had spoken.

Will wanted to punch the bastard in the nuts as he eyed Aubrey lasciviously and then licked his lips. "To the station in Cali central," he said.

Pierre was dead! How had this happened and when and what evidence did they have to say it was him?

"What about the girl—Camila?" he asked as they dragged him from the room to see Liam and Drew coming out of their rooms followed by Alex and Reid.

"There is no girl, just Mr Aubin," he stated as he stopped to glare at Alex who had his arms folded and was standing in the way of the police.

"What is going on?" he asked in quick-fire Spanish.

"Mr Granger is being charged with murder in the first degree for killing Pierre Aubin."

"On what evidence?" Alex asked.

"I am not at liberty to discuss this with you. Now please move, or I will be forced to see you as hostile and act accordingly," he responded, and the threat was clear.

"It's fine, Alex. Just meet me at the station and find me a lawyer," Will said as he looked at Aubrey. "I didn't do this, Aubrey," he stated, more worried that this would cause her to see all her fears as valid for why she wouldn't get involved with him.

"I know you didn't." She smiled, and he felt the first of a thousand knots in his gut loosen. He did, however, notice that his brother was conspicuous by his absence. Had he fucked up so bad that Jack had turned his back on him for good? The thought made his shoulders sag as they dragged him down the back stairs and shoved him into a police car that was parked at the back.

"Now, we will see what happens when you visitors," the policeman who was in charge sneered, "come to our country and interfere with things you know nothing about."

For the first time as Will looked around, he wondered how safe his life was and thanked God he still had his watch on him and that Drew could track him through it. Whether he ended up at the station or dead in a ditch was yet to be determined.

THE POUNDING in his head was like a bass drum as Jack pulled the pillow over his head and tried to drown out the noise that was making him feel like he wanted to puke his guts up. His mouth had fur all over the inside, and he felt like he had been sucking on a stone his gob was so dry.

What the fuck had happened last night to make him feel like this? Then he remembered Will—Eidolon—and his heart sunk. He couldn't remember all the details, just that lots had been said in anger and he couldn't remember much of it.

The door to his room crashed open. Jack sprung from the bed with his gun in his hand, pointing it at the door and his second in command who stood their glaring daggers at him. Jack dropped his arm and fell back on the bed, his arm over his eyes as his stomach lurched.

"Time to get the fuck up. No time to wallow in your misery. Will's in trouble and needs our help," Alex said as he started throwing clothes and shit at him.

Jack dropped his arm instantly and sat up, ignoring the throbbing behind his eyes and focused on Alex as he noticed the rest of his team behind him. "What do you mean in trouble?" he asked cautiously.

"Are you fuckin deaf now? Four cops just busted down Aubrey's door and arrested him for murder."

"Murder?" he asked confused.

"Yes. Get yourself up and showered while I make some coffee for your hungover ass," Alex said as he threw clothes at him and walked out slamming the door. Alex wasn't one to show his temper, so the fact that he was now was telling.

Moving into the bathroom, Jack stripped his dirty clothes from last night and stepped into a hot shower. He quickly washed the grime from his skin and shampooed his hair before rinsing and turning the shower to freezing to try and blow some of the cobwebs away.

What the hell had Will dragged them all into this time and why, even now, after everything, did he still want to run in and save his baby brother? He shivered as the cold hit him, but it had the desired effect of waking him the hell up.

He towelled off and dressed and was walking into the main part of the room when Liam let Aubrey in. They glared at each other before he dismissed her.

"Hey, asshole, don't give me that holier than thou look. If it weren't for you, Will would not even be here," she spat.

Jack stopped with the mug of coffee half way to his lips. "Excuse me?" he asked with incredulity. "Was it me he flew halfway around the world to save? Was it me that walked away without a fucking word? No. So either save your hissy fit for someone who cares or stay the fuck out of my way."

"Hey, hey let's take it down a notch," said Blake as he looked at Alex.

Jack didn't need to say more, he knew he had hit his mark with his words.

~

AUBREY FELT the weight of guilt on her shoulders at Jack's words. Ever since Will had been dragged away by that supercilious copper, she had felt it. The knowledge that if it weren't for her Will would be back in the UK safe, not in some Colombian jail accused of murder.

"No, Jack is right. Will is here because of me, and I'm going to make it right. Are you?" she challenged Jack.

"He's my brother, don't ever doubt that I will help him."

She saw the warning there. A warning meant for her and for the first time she actually liked Jack. He might be an arrogant asshole, but he loved his sibling and she could relate to that. "Fine tell me everything."

"Tell me everything," they both said and then looked at each other with a frown.

"Why don't you go first and tell me what just happened," Jack said.

"Fine. Will and I were fast asleep when the door was smashed in, and four armed police rushed in with guns pointing at Will. They said he was under arrest for the murder of Pierre Aubin. Then he was cuffed and dragged out. One of them hit him in the head with a baton when he struggled. We saw these guys in the hallway and Alex spoke to the dickwad that arrested him."

"Why were you in the hallway?" Jack asked, and Aubrey raised her eyebrows.

"Oh, I don't know, maybe because it sounded like world war three was breaking out!" Drew said, and Aubrey looked at him.

"Exactly," said Alex.

"What did you say to him?" Jack asked.

"I asked him what was going on and he said Will had been arrested on charges of murder. I asked what evidence they had, and he said he wasn't at liberty to discuss it," Alex said as he crossed his arms over his chest and rocked back on his heels.

"They said they were taking him to Cali Central Police Station," Aubrey added.

"Fine. Let's talk to our contact at the embassy and find out what they have. Also, find out about Pierre Aubin. Drew, you know Will's systems. Get in and find out whatever you can that will help. Check the CCTV footage with Blake. Reid, start asking questions from our sources here about Pierre Aubin. Because I'll be damned if my brother is going to rot in some godforsaken Colombian jail."

Aubrey was impressed by Jack's ability to go from having a killer hangover to taking charge, and she could see why Will trusted him to run Eidolon.

"What about me? I am a police detective you know," she said stating the obvious. She had no intention of being side-lined while her sister, and now Will, were in danger.

"You and I are going to the station, but first we need to find Will a lawyer and fast."

"Okay." She bit her lip not wanting to say it for fear of sounding like a heartless bitch over Will's plight.

"Spit it out," Jack rasped as he folded his arms and sighed.

"What about Madison? She's still with Chopper, and I don't trust him. She might be a thoughtless pain in the ass, but she is my sister, and I'll do anything to save her."

"Even sell out my brother?"

Aubrey thought her head was going to explode at his words. "What the fuck did you just accuse me off?" she asked as she stormed closer, so they were nose to nose.

"Well, it seems funny that my brother is obviously being set up and you're trying to free your sister. It would be the perfect deal for Chopper to get rid of Will and fuck us over at the same time. It could be argued you would do that for your sister."

"You are the biggest prick I have ever met," she said and continued to glare.

"So I've been told." He shrugged.

"Will you two pack it the fuck in and come look at this," shouted Drew who was already working at the laptop.

Aubrey glared a Jack one more time before moving to Drew. "What is it?" she asked as she looked over his shoulder.

What she saw made her heart drop.

CHAPTER 11

"How is that possible? Will was here when this happened. If you look at the time stamp you can see." The image on the screen showed a clear picture of Will as he pointed a gun at who she assumed to be Pierre Aubin and fired. The man fell to the ground dead. "Pull up all the CCTV from the hotel," Aubrey demanded trying not to let her fear for Will show in her voice.

They all waited in silence, the only sound Drew's fingers as they flew over the keys. "The only footage I can find is of Will leaving the hotel through the back stairs around ten. That must be just after he left you at the bar," Drew said looking at Liam.

"Yes, that's right. He got a phone call just before and then left almost immediately afterwards," replied Liam as he clicked his fingers and paced.

"Find Will's phone. I want to know who called him," Jack demanded of Blake, who immediately left to do as he had been asked.

"What else do you have?" Aubrey asked Drew.

"Nothing. Everything else has been wiped," he stated as he looked up at her from his seat.

"Fuck!" growled Jack.

"That's not all," Drew said with a frown. "Will's watch just went offline. But his last ping wasn't at Cali Central."

"Where was it?" asked Aubrey as her stomach knotted tight. This was all wrong, and she had an incredibly bad feeling about it.

"Headed towards East Cali in the Aguablanca district."

"Oh, this is not good news," said Alex. "Aguablanca is a no-go for foreigners and not safe at all. It is run by the Rojas Cartel. We need to locate Will and extract him as soon as possible."

"I agree. The chances that this is a regular arrest just flew out the window," Jack replied. "Forget the lawyer, we won't need one. Drew, see if you can pick up any sign of Will on any cameras and monitor the watch. What was his health like when it went off?"

"Health? What the hell do you mean?" Aubrey asked confused.

"The watches Will designed monitor vital signs like BP, pulse rate, and oxygen saturation. It can give us a picture of his health based on the readings," Jack said, and Aubrey wondered if he could hear the pride in his voice as clearly as the rest of them could. The relationship between the brothers was damaged, but it wasn't dead. She was still simmering over Jack's accusation of her selling Will out, but she would let it go for now.

"Wow, that's very clever. So, what was his health reading?" she asked Drew.

"He was stable when it last pinged which is good news."

"I have an appointment with a woman at the embassy in thirty minutes," said Blake who had just walked in with Will's phone. He handed the phone to Jack who accessed it in seconds and checked the call log.

"He had a call from inside the embassy at twenty-one fifty-five and it lasted maybe two minutes," he said out loud.

"That must be it," Liam agreed.

"Blake, take Drew and Liam with you. I want Drew to hack the embassy and find out which terminal this came from. It's more than likely Pierre Aubin but let's check and then interview the head of security and find out if they've had any new hires lately. If someone is setting my brother up for murder, then we start there. Reid and Alex,

I want you to continue with the mission to bring Madison Herbert home safely," he stated, and Aubrey felt relief flood her.

"What about me? Shouldn't I help Alex and Reid?" Aubrey asked almost daring him to accuse her again.

Jack looked at her with a tilt of his head. "We're headed to East Cali, so if you aren't up for this then say so. I won't have you dragging me back on this."

"I can handle myself but why take me?" she deadpanned not rising to his bait.

"Because I don't trust you and I want you where I can keep an eye on you."

"You know, we are very similar," she said.

Jack quirked an eyebrow at her but didn't say anything. "Let's go," he replied.

Aubrey was silent as she followed him to the vehicles in the parking lot behind the hotel.

∼

WILL FELL to his knees as they pushed him into a damp, dirty room that contained a small metal table that was bolted to the ground and three chairs. There were no windows, and the walls were made of thick concrete.

"Take it easy, asshole," he growled at the policeman who had led him inside. That got him a kick to the guts that stole the breath from his lungs. He let out a chuckle knowing that it would do him no good to show the fear he felt inside.

He had dealt with bullies in juvie and to show any fear or weakness was to put a target on his back. Well, in this case, a bigger target. Someone was already setting him up, and he just needed to figure out a way to find out who.

He watched as the policeman left and locked the door before he got to his feet then sat in the chair with his back to the wall. He would not show these people his back, or they would more than likely put a knife in it.

They had taken off his watch when they had stopped off at a barrio on the way to the East Cali police station. The man who had arrested him had gone in when a woman who looked suspiciously like Camila had opened the door. He hadn't been able to see clearly from where he sat in the back of the car, but as she looked at the vehicle surreptitiously, he had thought it was her.

The door to the room opened, and Will looked up, letting his face go blank.

"Mr Granger, you will shortly be charged with the murder of Pierre Aubin, but before that, we have someone who would like to meet you."

"What evidence do you have against me?" he asked needing to know how flimsy this was or how much effort had been put into setting him up. It would give him a better idea of who he was dealing with. He knew Jack and the team would be coming for him. It didn't matter how they fell out Jack would not walk away and leave him here, it just wasn't in him.

"Ah, Mr Granger, what makes you think you are in a position to ask questions? You foreigners are all the same, thinking it is your right when all you do is interfere with things you don't understand."

Will said nothing knowing that silence was more likely to rattle him than arguing would. He was right and a beat later he started getting the answers he sought.

"We have CCTV that captures you putting a bullet in the head of poor Mr Aubin. Unfortunately, this has already been leaked to the internet," he said with mock regret.

Will clenched his jaw in silence knowing that his friends and family—including his mother—may have seen it. Worse, his father might have.

"What about Camila Perez?" he asked instead, trying to get a read if she was part of this or not.

"Who? I have not heard of such a woman. Who was she?"

"Pierre Aubin's girlfriend," he responded.

The smug officer gave a dismissive sound as he pursed his lips and shrugged his shoulder. "Mr Aubin did not have a girlfriend as far as our enquiries show, but he did have some high connections with the cartel, and I understand they are pretty keen to meet you since you murdered their best accountant."

"Accountant? Pierre worked for the embassy."

"And what better cover than working for the British Embassy. Pierre Aubin was the top accountant for Santiago Rojas, and now he is dead by your hand, they want you to fill his shoes."

"Well, that doesn't sound like a dedicated officer of the law," Will sneered.

"Maybe not but the rules are different here, and we do what we must."

"Including setting up innocent people?" Will asked knowing that he would never see the inside of a courtroom—this was a ruse to get him to do the cartel's bidding.

"You are no innocent, Mr Granger, your time in prison proves that."

"And how do you know about that?" Will asked carefully, knowing those records were sealed tight, and the only way anyone could have found out was they either hacked them, which meant that they were good, or that they knew to look for them. He'd made no secret amongst his friends about what he had done, but it wasn't public knowledge anymore. He didn't want his past to effect Fortis or Eidolon.

"We all have our contacts, Mr Granger, and our enemies," he added slyly.

So, Will had an enemy he didn't know about? Not surprising really but one that would go to these lengths for revenge? That was more unusual.

"So it seems. How did you know I was in Miss Herbert's room?" he asked the question that had been niggling him.

"As I said before, we all have our contacts, Mr Granger and some of them are better behind a keyboard than even you," he said with a sneer which Will ignored.

"So, I'm being taken to the cartel?" he said changing tactic.

"Yes, but not until much later tonight. For now, you will remain here while your little team scrabbles to find you." He laughed as he stood to leave.

"They will find me and when they do, they will kill you," Will said. He held eye contact with the man who walked towards him slowly, his confidence and swagger at odds with his beer belly.

"I do not fear the likes of you and your team. You are dealing with men that have no hesitation in killing just because they can. That is power, and that is what you will never understand."

"You are wrong. I understand power and influence and the seductive power it has, but I have something more. I have a family, and I have loyalty."

"My men are loyal," he blustered, his face going red.

"Are they though?" Will asked calmly.

"Do not question my men or my authority," he bellowed, and Will saw the blow coming as he was punched repeatedly in the face. He didn't murmur or make a sound but simply spat out the blood from his mouth as he glared at the bent copper who was breathing hard.

He had hit his mark, and he knew this man would be watching those around him more carefully for the remainder of the day. That would give him some peace, he hoped, to figure out which of the two men he could identify as his enemy had set him up. His cellmate from juvie or his father.

CHAPTER 12

They were halfway to Cali East when they got a call from Alex to say they had info from the embassy. Jack put the call on speaker phone, so she could hear, and Aubrey was pleased this would not be one long battle as her nerves were already frayed.

"Go ahead, Alex, I have you on speaker," Jack said as he drove.

"I just heard back from Blake, and he says the call came from Pierre Aubin's office. Drew also managed to get in and download all the files on Aubin's computer. He's bringing them back here to go through them now, but it seems Pierre Aubin was working for the Rojas Cartel. I've asked Drew to tear Aubin's life apart, and Lucy is helping on that front from the UK. Oh, and FYI Zack is on the warpath because you never told him, and that he, and I quote, 'had to find out through fucking YouTube'."

"Yeah, yeah, I'll call him," said Jack with a roll of his eyes. "What else?"

"Blake found out they've had three new members of staff in the last three months, all British Nationals. I've asked Lucy to go through them and see if she can find anything."

"Good, anything else?" Jack asked impatiently.

"Yes, there's some chatter that the cartel is bringing in a new recruit to handle their digital accounting," Alex said.

Aubrey felt her stomach twist. "Will," she breathed.

"Yes, my guess is this is all an elaborate way to discredit Will so that when he drops off the radar, nobody comes looking. They'll think he's gone on the run."

"But if this person is intelligent enough to do all this, surely they would figure you would come for him?" Aubrey asked looking at Jack.

"Maybe they don't know. Will's link to us is hidden, as is all his other work."

"Fortis then?" she asked.

"Maybe but either way we need to get him out before he's taken to Rojas, as getting him out of their compound will be a nightmare."

"We take him on the road?" Aubrey asked, and Jack raised an eyebrow in surprise.

"That's the best option," Alex added.

"Fine, we'll do some recon. Leave Drew and Blake on that and you, Reid, and Liam meet me at the coordinates I'm sending you. We can plan a moving takedown. I doubt they'll move him before, so we have a few hours."

"Copy that," Alex said and hung up.

Jack continued to drive in silence as Aubrey watched the landscape go past. Her brain played over every titbit of information she had about this case and about Will. That invariably led to how she felt about him. She had promised Jack she would stay away from his brother, but it was one she was going to break. She wondered about the dynamic between the brothers. There was obviously a lot of love, but there was also a lot of tension, and she wondered where it came from. Maybe now was the perfect time to do a little digging of her own.

"So, Will's your boss, bet that didn't go down very well," she said opening the topic in a slightly confrontational manner.

Jack swung his gaze to hers, a slight look of surprise on his face that she would go there. When he looked back to the road, she thought he wouldn't answer so was surprised when he did. "Will being my boss isn't the problem, it's the lying I can't forgive."

"Have you thought perhaps he had a good reason to lie?"

"There is never a good reason to lie to family," he snapped.

"I disagree. Lies are not always told to hurt. Sometimes, they are told to protect."

"Look, I'm not an idiot. I know life isn't black and white, and shit happens, but Will and I were close as kids. We didn't fight or get jealous, but then he pulled away from me and started hiding stuff. Then when he hacked that bank, I felt like I'd lost my kid brother and I don't know why I'm oversharing with you," he finished with a snort and shake of his head.

Aubrey smiled then, thinking perhaps Jack wasn't such an asshole after all. "Maybe you two should talk, I mean really talk. It's never too late you know. Will hero worships you."

He glanced at her again as he slowed the car as the road became bumpy. "He might have once, but he barely tolerates me these days."

"You are so wrong. Will misses you."

"You really like him, don't you?" he asked changing the subject.

Aubrey didn't know what to say for a second, but as she had just lectured him on honesty, perhaps a spoonful of her own medicine was in order. "I do, yes. He's sweet, funny, obviously gorgeous."

"If you like tattooed geeks, I guess," Jack replied, and Aubrey saw the fun behind the zipped up man.

"He makes me feel special," she answered with a shy smile.

"So why did you run?"

"Because he scares me."

Jack looked at her sharply then. "Will would never hurt anyone, he doesn't have it in him," Jack defended.

"I know that he would never hurt me on purpose but what if by letting go and loving him, I get hurt?"

"No guts, no glory," he replied.

"So, does this mean I have your blessing?" she said and laughed.

"Jury is still out. How about we get this shit sorted with Will and Madison and then I'll let you know," he replied.

"Deal, and you have to give Will a chance to explain."

"Deal," he said slowing as they got closer into Aguablanca. He pulled in to the carpark of a deserted strip mall but kept the engine running. They couldn't afford to stay long and attract attention.

"We need to find out which road out they're going to take," Jack said pulling out a small tablet and bringing up a map.

"If it were me taking Will, I'd use the back road that runs along the edge of the jungle line," Aubrey said pointing to the road that arced around the village and headed back towards Cali.

He looked at her and nodded. "Yes, I agree. As soon as the others arrive, we'll plan it and get Alex and Reid to run the route."

Aubrey nodded and looked back towards the police station. "Do you think he's alright?"

"Yeah. Will is a tough bastard, and he's savvy. He knows how to handle people like that."

"Yeah, I guess. I just hate the thought of him being set up."

"You seem more worried about Will than Madison," Jack said, and Aubrey looked at him sharply waiting for the judgement but found none.

She sighed in frustration. "Madison has been getting into scrapes all our lives, so I think I'm desensitised to her shit now. Of course, I *am* worried, but it's tempered by anger at her blatant disregard for her own safety and my feelings."

"I get that, that's how I feel about Will." He nodded sadly. "Maybe we both have some big discussions in our future," he said with a shrug.

"Maybe?" she answered without committing.

∼

DARKNESS WAS DESCENDING by the time they had finalised the plan and confirmed through the text chatter they had picked up from different sources that Will was being picked up by Esteban Perez and his men.

Knowing that Esteban was doing the collection changed little except the value the cartel placed on Will. Esteban was Santiago

Rojas' right-hand man, and he never left his side. They had thought they would get a lower level soldier involved for this but Esteban doing it showed how much they wanted Will and that scared Aubrey.

They'd set up a takedown on the abandoned road that spurred off towards derelict farmlands. Keeping everything on the down-low was a priority, and the last thing they wanted was random involvement from young men looking to impress the cartel by shooting at them.

Liam had set charges to take out the lead vehicle as they had suspected that they would use a three-car convoy for the job. Then Reid and Jack could take out the drivers from the principle car and rear vehicle. She and Alex would provide cover from slightly further out.

As they drove to the target point, Aubrey went over the plan again in her head. She was to watch Jack, Reid, and Liam's six along with Alex. They had shocked her when they had included her in the plan. Aubrey had kept up firearms training with the hope of one day getting into the Firearms Unit on the London Met.

That dream didn't have the pull it once did, but she enjoyed the firearms practice immensely so kept it up. The only thing she didn't know was how Jack had known she was so proficient with a firearm.

It was dark when the car she was in stopped and she and Alex got out, grabbed their weapons and disappeared into the darkness as the others drove on. Finding some scrub to use as cover she flattened herself along the ground in silence as Alex did the same a few feet to the left of her.

"Comms check," came over the mike and she responded.

"Alpha five checking in," she replied when the others had spoken.

The comm went silent as they waited, her heart was beating a steady tattoo as Aubrey focused on what she had to do. The cold night air bit into her skin as the heat from the earth gave way to the cold of the night. It had taken a few minutes to get her head around the night vision goggles Liam had given her, but she was fine now.

"Alpha one, this is alpha three. We have three incoming vehicles approximately a mile out, but they are not cartel. Repeat, not cartel.

My contact says the men who picked up Will were not cartel but private security mercenaries."

"Copy that, alpha three. Continue as planned but prepare for this to get ugly. Looks like the dirty bastard has his hands in this pie too."

Aubrey had no idea who or what they meant, but she knew it wasn't good. Her adrenalin was pumping, her heart beating faster as they waited, the only sounds that of bugs and animals from the jungle in the distance.

Soon she heard vehicles and saw the dust start to kick up as they rounded the corners.

"Alpha one, this is alpha two. Confirm that the target is on board in the right rear seat with a man beside him. Chopper is in the third car."

Aubrey gasped, and it was now abundantly clear who they had been talking about. Chopper was more involved with the cartel than they realised if he had been charged with this job.

"Keep a clear head," Alex warned from next to her.

The vehicle came into view, and as the first vehicle passed the checkpoint, she waited a second before the explosion came. The vehicle lifted into the air as it flipped over and over, taking out that threat. Reid and Jack fired almost simultaneously and the second and third cars swerved as the drivers were taken out. Aubrey watched as the second car came to a rolling stop and the doors opened. Shots were fired instantly and then returned by Jack and Reid. The back door opened, and she saw Will pushed out face first before a hail of fire rained down on the person firing at Reid and Jack.

Two men from the third car were crouched low as they fired at Jack currently running towards an unmoving Will who was lying prone on the ground. Aubrey watched as the two men fell, hearing the discharge of a weapon beside her as Alex covered Jack and Will. Jack reached Will and fell to his knees beside him. Her heart almost stopped as she watched Jack lift his brother, hoisting him over his shoulder, before running for cover.

Liam joined him running backwards as he covered his friend. She saw Chopper try to run away and took aim through the scope. Her finger hovered over the trigger as she watched him move further away and she realised with horror that she couldn't do it. She couldn't do what these men did with such ease.

In that minute she wished with all her heart that she could, but it wasn't her. She was a cop, sure but she couldn't kill someone. She watched as he ran to the road and was picked up on a motorbike that sped away in the opposite direction. She felt a firm hand on her shoulder and looked up.

"It's okay, let him go. There will be other opportunities to finish this," Alex said kindly.

"But I'm meant to be covering them, and I failed. I could have gotten them killed."

"You did not fail, I had it covered. Killing is not something that should ever be done lightly and is not something many can do. It takes a piece of you every time you do it, so please, do not berate yourself for being the person who can't." He held out his hand and helped her up as they moved down towards the cars and the dead men side by side. She wondered if Alex was just being kind and Jack would chew her out, but she needn't have.

The instant she saw Jack talking to Will in the back of the car she took off running and didn't stop until she was in his arms.

His arms came around her and held her tight as she buried her nose in his neck, running her hands all over him to make sure he was okay. "Are you alright? Did they hurt you?" she asked pulling back and wincing when she saw his face. His eye was black and swollen, his lip split, but he still looked perfect to her.

"I'm fine," he said with a lopsided grin and a wink.

"Let's get out of here before they come back with more men," Jack said as Reid pulled up in their vehicle.

Liam came over with a handful of weapons, phones, and knives he had apparently taken off the bodies. Aubrey helped Will walk and realised he was moving gingerly from pain and that she probably hadn't helped when she'd launched herself at him, but she had acted on instinct. Her need to touch him far outweighed anything else.

It was in that moment that she realised that whatever else

happened she would give Will a chance, give them a chance. She had thought she had known how fragile life was losing her parents but watching these men fight for one of their own, kill and risk being killed, it had suddenly hit home that in a split second everything could change. Will could have died, and she would have lived with a lifetime more regret that she did already.

Slipping her hand in his, she smiled when he gave it a light squeeze and winked at her. They would get through this and see what happened. Maybe the future could be sweet if they lived long enough to see it.

CHAPTER 13

They had arrived at the safehouse Jack had somehow managed to secure in Buga. It was over an hour away from Cali and had a large enough tourist population that they could get lost in it. The house was about two miles out of town and surrounded by lush fields of arabica plants. The house had belonged to a corrupt official that had died when the last cartel in Cali had been overthrown by Rojas.

This home had been sold to someone in the US who used it as a holiday home now that Buga was not infected by cartel filth so much. The owner was one of the many contacts Jack, and his men, had engineered over the years—both before Eidolon had formed and since.

The home itself had five big bedrooms all with an en-suite and a large, open plan living area and kitchen. A large patio and BBQ area led down to a pool and deck.

"Let me clean that face of yours up," Aubrey said as they stepped through them into the living room.

"It's fine. I can do it when I shower. I stink and want to get cleaned up," Will replied not wanting to bother her.

"Never could do as he was told," sniped Jack.

Will looked up sharply ready to tell him to lay off, that he was too tired for this shit. But Jack was grinning, and for the first time in what felt like years, he saw the older brother who had built Lego with him. He looked away before Jack caught his eye, afraid he would see the relief on his face. "No, I guess not," he answered instead. "How about I shower, and then you can do all the fixing up I need?" he said to Aubrey.

She put her hands on her hips and tilted her head as she regarded him. "Okay but only because you do actually stink." She laughed and then dove out the way when his eyebrow shot to his hairline.

"You're going to pay for that," he said before he sobered. "Do we know any more on who set me up and killed Pierre?" he asked directing his question at Jack.

"We know that Santiago Rojas wanted you to fill his shoes. We know that Pierre was working for them but other than that we don't have much." The outside door opened, and Drew walked in followed by Jace.

"Hey, man, what are you doing here?" Will asked as he strode over to his cousin and embraced him, giving him a hard slap on the back.

"Thought I had better get my ass over here and help you out, so Ma didn't get on the phone and start in at me," Jace said with a chuckle.

"I called him. We're a few men short, and I need Reid and Blake to go after Madison now I have intel on where she is."

"You do?" Aubrey asked surprised. "Why didn't you tell me?"

"Because you didn't need to know," Jack responded with a sigh as he crossed his arms.

"Because you still don't trust me?" she asked with indignation as she glared at his brother.

Will got a distinct impression that there was more going on here but kept quiet as it played out.

"Trust is hard to come by and easily broken, so no, I don't trust you, but don't take it personally. I can count on one hand how many people I truly trust," Jack answered before he walked outside to talk to Liam and Alex. Drew headed back out to get the laptops he guessed.

"That man is an asshole," Aubrey spat as she stormed from the room towards the bedroom she was using.

"Still the same drama following you then," Jace said with a grin as he dropped his bag beside the sofa.

"Yeah, I should probably go find out what all that was about."

"You think?" said Jace with a shake of his head.

"Yeah," Will replied absentmindedly. "Hey, has Lucy found out anything?" he asked as he got to the door and turned back towards his cousin.

Jace was already filling up the coffee pot. "She had a lead when I left, but she's calling me in a few minutes and I'll ask her then. Don't worry, Will, we're going to work this out."

"I know. Thanks, Jace."

"It's what family does man," he said.

Yeah, they did, thought Will as he passed the room Aubrey was using and stopped for a second. Maybe he should check on her, but as he moved, he caught a whiff of his armpits and thought perhaps a shower first, then he could hold her as he so desperately wanted to.

Grabbing clean jeans and a white polo from the bag that had mysteriously appeared on the bed, he headed for the bathroom. Stripping his clothes, he bunched them up and shoved them in a bin bag ready to burn. The bathroom was tiled entirely in white from floor to ceiling and bright green towels were hung on the silver, heated towel rail.

Stepping under the hot spray, Will let it run over him, feeling the bite as the water hit the cuts on his face. He had been shocked to see Chopper, but as he had never dealt with him in the forces, he didn't know him that well.

He went over in his mind what had been said to look for a clue. Something was niggling him, and it was just out of his grasp. Chopper hadn't said a lot, but it was more his mannerisms than what was said. He had referred to Jack and how important family was. Will couldn't make out if he was trying to ruffle him or if it was just a threat that if he didn't do as he was told, he would go after Jack.

Will had no worries that Jack could handle himself though. He was the best, probably better than Zack in some ways because he didn't allow feelings to get in the way. Yet he had come for him, even after the way things had been left.

Deciding that standing in the shower all day would accomplish exactly nothing, Will got out and wrapped a towel around his waist. Looking in the mirror over the sink he saw that his eye looked better already now the dry blood was cleaned away. Opening the bathroom door, he stopped short when he saw Aubrey standing in the middle of his room looking uncertain.

"Aubrey?" he asked as he went closer to her.

She had her hands clasped in front of her. She had changed into a blue tank top and denim shorts, her legs went on for miles, toned muscle and perfectly shaped. He dragged his eyes up and over her curves as he felt his body start to respond and remembered he was in a towel. He closed his eyes and began to recite code in his head to get the picture of her naked and beneath him from his brain. When he felt he had himself under control, he opened them, and she was looking at him with a twitch on her lips.

"I knocked, but you didn't answer, so I let myself in. I probably shouldn't have," she said with a hesitancy he was not used to from her.

"What's going on, Brey?" he asked, and her eyes flashed to him in surprise at his shortening of her name.

"Nobody calls me that!" she stated.

"Yeah, but I'm not nobody am I?" he replied as he moved closer and her eyes dropped to his body. Will saw desire darken the brown of her eyes to almost black and fought for control, he wanted to hold her, touch her, make her scream his name as he tasted her.

"No, you're not 'nobody', Will."

He moved a step closer and lifted his hand to stroke the pulse in her neck. Goosebumps rose on her skin, and he saw her shiver, her lips part on a breath. "What are we, Brey?" he asked as he cupped the back of her neck with his hand and ran his nose over the soft shell of her ear, delighting in the sensation of her so close.

He wanted to devour her, worship her but first, he needed her to admit they were something special.

"We're good friends," she answered, and he felt the disappointment burn.

He opened his eyes and stepped back from her, fighting the pull to just say fuck it, but he needed her to come to him this time. "Wrong answer, Brey," he said as he turned his back on her and grabbed his jeans from the bed. The bed which he could have made her scream in.

"Will," she said sounding frustrated, and his lips twitched, knowing that she was suffering too.

"Are you going to watch me dress? I'm pretty sure friends don't do that," he said with a sarcastic tone.

"Don't be a dick. You said we could go slow."

"And you said we would try."

"I know, but I'm scared, Will," she admitted, and instantly his anger left, and he felt like an asshole.

He dropped the jeans on the bed and turned to her, she looked lost, and he hated it. Will pushed a hand through his dark hair and took a deep breath. "You're right, I'm sorry," he relented and saw her smile.

"Did that hurt?"

"Yes, want to kiss it better?" he asked with a smile as she moved to him.

"Yes, but not right now. We need to find out what is going on, so we can clear your name and then you need to talk to Jack. You two are so screwed up it isn't funny."

He grabbed the jeans and walked to the bathroom as she spoke, determined to put some clothes on lest he embarrass himself with this towel. He left the door open a smidge as he carried on their conversation. "Yeah, what was all that about with Jack?"

"Oh, nothing. He just thought I had set you up in exchange for Madison," she said with no anger in her voice now.

"He what?" he bellowed as he came out pulling the t-shirt over his head and catching her ogling him. He winked and smirked, and she blushed making his smile widen. He moved to her taking her hands as he looked at her intently. "Want me to have a word with him?" he asked not wanting to step on her toes.

"No, I've calmed down now and honestly, had it been the other way around, I'm not sure I wouldn't have drawn the same conclusion."

"Jack can be a bit intense," Will said trying to defend his brother.

"He loves you, Will. He's just trying to protect you. I don't know everything that went on between you two, but I know there's a lot that should have been said and hasn't."

"You're right but I'm not sure if it is too late."

"He's still here isn't he?" Aubrey moved closer and cupped his jaw with her soft, smooth hands. "You are a good man, Will. I've met a lot of bad men, a lot of men only out for themselves, and that's not you. I don't know why you did what you did when you were younger, but I know you had a good reason. One day, I hope you will share that with me, but the most important person is you, and I know you miss Jack, so tell him. He might be an asshole, but he loves you." She was impassioned with her words, taking his breath away for the second time.

"When did you get so wise?" he asked instead.

"I'm not, or maybe I would take my own advice," she replied. He knew she was thinking of her sister. "Yeah maybe we both should, but one thing at a time let's get you cleared and go home."

He wrapped an arm around her shoulder and pulled her in close as they moved to the door. "Let's go kick some butt," he replied as he kissed her head inhaling the scent of her shampoo. This woman was his in every way, he just had to convince her of that, but he had made progress, and that was all he could ask.

CHAPTER 14

THE SMELL OF SOMETHING DELICIOUS HIT HER NOSE AS SOON AS SHE walked into the open plan kitchen and her stomach rumbled loudly.

"Something smells good," said Will from beside her as he walked towards Alex who was stirring something in a pan. She followed close behind and tried to peer around Will as he stood next to Alex.

"What you cooking?" Will asked and tried to dip a spoon he had snagged from the side into the dark red meaty mixture.

"If you put that spoon in there, I'll stab you in the eye with it," Alex growled as he glared at Will.

"Hey, cool down. How long until we eat? I'm starving," Will asked putting the spoon down and backing away with his hands in the air.

"About thirty minutes or so," Alex said as he winked at her and grinned before turning his glare back on Will.

"Fine, so time for some hacking. Where is everyone?"

"They went to shower."

"Do you need any help?" Aubrey asked looking around the kitchen area.

"No, I'm good thanks. Go relax," Alex replied as he added more spice to the mixture that was making her mouth water.

She wandered over to Will who was sitting with his laptop open, already typing at a furious pace. She sat down next to him on the couch and curled her right leg under her left as she watched code fly across the screen. "What are you doing?" she asked, in awe with his skill on a computer.

"I'm hacking into the embassy to see if I can access Pierre's computer."

"Oh, I should have said, Drew downloaded that," she said as Will glanced at her and winked.

"I know, but he wouldn't have gotten all the deleted files."

"How did you get into this? Hacking and everything?" she asked, wanting to know the man behind the ink.

"I always had a head for numbers even as a young kid. I loved anything to do with numbers and I was lucky my math teacher saw it and introduced me to computers and coding. By the time I was eleven, I had written and sold my first programme," he said with a shrug as if what he could do was nothing special.

"Wow, Will, that is awesome. What are some of the programmes you've written?" she asked and was surprised when Will blushed.

"I wrote a programme that helps kids with dyslexia when I was fifteen. I wrote a programme that helps detect microbes and dangerous pathogens in river water and then filters it accordingly when I was twenty-two. Oh, and I wrote one that detects if a young person will develop dementia by analysing brain waves and patterns last year."

Aubrey could do nothing but stare at him open-mouthed as he listed all the amazing things he had done with no intent to show off. To Will, what he did was nothing, it was like her solving a simple speeding offence.

"You have no clue how amazing you are, do you?" she said with a smile as his face reddened.

"It isn't a big deal to me. I see code the way other people can read a book. It comes easy to me, so if I can do good with it, then I want to," he replied giving her his full attention.

"Which makes me wonder why you hacked that bank." Aubrey

watched as his eyes went stormy with pain. "It doesn't ring true, Will. It doesn't add up, and I want to know why."

"Sometimes things just happen," he said looking away.

Aubrey took his hand and brought it to her lap. "No, I don't believe that. The man that invented a programme to help dyslexic kids does not just turn around and hack a bank. Why won't you tell me the truth?"

"Because the truth will hurt too many people," he replied pulling his hand away and turning back to the screen. Aubrey dropped the subject as the rest of the team started to filter into the room.

"Is that Ropa Vieja?" Drew asked as he headed towards Alex.

"Yes, it is, how did you know that?"

"I like to eat," he answered as if that was an answer in itself.

Alex seemed to accept that as he began to serve up. Aubrey looked away as Jack walked towards them, his hands in his pockets.

"Find anything?" he asked as he looked at Will.

"Maybe. Pierre had a hidden bank account that the idiot was accessing through his work computer. It shows that he was getting money from a Manx account."

"Isn't that where Rhea Winslow had a home?" Jack asked, moving closer to look over Will's shoulder.

"Yes, but it isn't tracing back to her as far as I can see, but I'll keep digging."

"Fine, we need to figure out who might have the skills to set you up with doctoring the CCTV and would want to. I also have questions regarding Chopper. Can we talk after dinner?" Jack asked, and Aubrey was pleased to see that there was less animosity than before.

"Yeah, we can talk over dinner if you like, that way I can tell everyone together."

"Fine but I do need to talk to you on our own in private afterwards."

"Yeah, sure. Sounds good," said Will looking up at his brother with so much regret that Aubrey had to swallow the tears at the pain she saw between the two men. She dearly hoped they could work out their differences because they needed each other now more than ever.

Dinner was a loud affair, but it was more fun than she could remember having in years. Eidolon was a family as much as Jack, Will, and Jace were actual family. Alex, she was surprised but happy to realise, was a fantastic cook, and she had told him so.

"Everyone wants the long-term missions with Alex because of his cooking," said Liam, "but don't get stuck with Decker. That man can burn water."

"So how did you guys all meet?" she asked realising this may be a delicate subject and not caring. This, whatever it was needed to come, and she wasn't above pushing it. She saw Jace glance at Jack and Will with a cautious eye. Jack went still, his fork halfway to his mouth. Will glanced at her in the silence, his face warning her not to push it.

"I met most of these men through my time in the forces. Decker, Liam, and Ambrose were recommendations from Zack who I had served with before I was fired."

"Jack!" Jace said with a frown.

Jack cast him a look before looking to Will with accusation. "What don't tell Aubrey how Will got me fired from my dream job in the SAS because he left evidence that pointed towards my involvement in the bank hack?" he said, his face red as he pushed back angrily from the table.

"It wasn't like that, Jack," Will defended quietly.

Aubrey could see the conflict on his face when she looked at him and regretted opening this up. Maybe now was not the time to force Will to show the man she knew was buried under years of guilt. A good man, a kind man, one who loved his family and friends more than he ever let on.

"Then what was it like, Will, because I would really like to know what the fuck I ever did to you to cause you to lie, and fuck me over like you did?" Jack asked as the table went silent, the energy in the room was so tense it was making her head hurt.

Aubrey stood and moved to stand behind Will, showing her support and hoping that he would speak to her after this.

"Got nothing to say?" Jack asked as he glared at his brother. "No, I didn't think so," he spat as he turned and strode from the room.

Aubrey felt the eyes of the men on her but couldn't look at them, her focus solely on Will. She reached a hand out to him as the men began to murmur around them. "Will?" she asked unsure of his response.

He looked up at her with disappointment and sadness in his eyes. "It's okay, Aubrey, it had to happen," he responded grasping her hand and placing a kiss on her palm.

"Do you want me to go and explain this was my fault?" she asked not relishing the thought of facing Jack but willing to anyway.

He shook his head. "No, this is long overdue and my problem. I'll go but do me a favour?"

"Of course," she answered instantly.

"Save me some of that rice pudding Alex is pulling out of the oven," he said as he rubbed her cheek with his thumb and stood before dropping a kiss on her head.

"Consider it done," she said with a smile.

Aubrey watched as Will walked outside the way his brother had gone, and she prayed she hadn't made a colossal error in judgement.

She sat at the table in Will's seat and fought with the desire to go and fix this mess, but she knew it wasn't hers to fix. Maybe that was half her problem, she'd spent her entire life trying to make amends for something she hadn't done.

Her thoughts went to Mickey for the first time in years. Will reminded her of Mickey so much, she knew it was why she had pushed Will away. They had both had the same sweetness to them that was shrouded in a bad boy persona. Her mind drifted back to the night of the fire, how special she had felt with Mickey and then the look on his face when he had seen her home as it burned, taking the lives of her parents and her childish dreams with it.

"Aubrey?" She looked up as Jace said her name. "It will be okay you know. This should have happened years ago," he said with sincerity and no sign of judgement.

"Thank you. I was just trying to help," she replied. "Will is a good man, and I hate to see him hurting," she offered as a way of explanation.

"You like him." He'd said it as a statement, not a question.

"Yes, I do, a lot but he has so many secrets," she said as she worried her hands in her lap.

"We all do, but they don't define us as people and you're right about one thing. Will is a good man and so is Jack, and I don't just say that because we're family, I say it because it's true. Luce adores Will. You know he once flew all the way to Brazil to spend her birthday with her because she was missing her family and couldn't get home. He took her dancing and then flew home the next day. Those are the kinds of things he does for those he cares about, and he never says a word. I don't think Dane knows to this day that he did that for Luce."

"Why doesn't he tell anyone what he's doing?" she asked sadly as more of Will's goodness came to light.

"Because that's not who he is and when you grow up with a father that thinks kindness is a weakness, you tend to hide that side of yourself," Jace said through a gritted jaw.

As tempted as she was to ask about his father, she didn't. If Will wanted to tell her he would. "Thank you for telling me, and I promise Dane won't hear it from me."

She realised they were the only ones left at the table and stood. "We should get to work on exonerating Will. Do you think they have a marker around here somewhere? I could really use a visual and that large glass window would make the perfect murder board."

"Let's go find out," Jace said as he too stood.

Aubrey could see what Lucy loved about Jace. He was a solid support and level-headed with it, and he clearly adored the bones of Lucy. As they passed the door that led to the pool area, she saw Will and Jack were sitting on loungers facing each other, deep in conversation. She hoped that they could make peace out here amongst the hell around them.

CHAPTER 15

Stepping out into late night air, Will took in a fortifying breath before he approached Jack who was facing away from him. The breeze carrying the scent from the acacia plants caught the air, bringing with it the sounds of the night. He saw Jack's back stiffen when he heard him, but he didn't turn, and he wondered at the skills his brother possessed, the innate ability to feel tension and vibes and yet be so blind to what had been going on at home.

Steeping up beside him, he stopped as they both looked out over the vista below. The house had the perfect view of the town while still maintaining the protection of the plants that surrounded them. Neither man spoke as they preserved the delicate balance of peace before the pandora's box was opened and could never be closed again.

Will looked towards the stars that seemed so much brighter in this part of the world and the moon that seemed close enough to touch if he only reached for it. "Do you remember when we were kids and you would tell me that every time I lied, a puppy died?" Will asked not looking at his brother.

Jack gave a short, derisive chuckle before he answered. "Yeah, and every time you got caught in a lie you would cry," Jack responded.

"Yeah, I did but not for the reason you think, but because I could see in your eyes how disappointed you were," Will said and turned to face Jack at the same time Jack confronted him.

"And yet you got so good at it," he said, and Will saw the pain his lies had caused and knew he had to create more pain for his brother by breaking the cycle of lies in his family.

"When I was fifteen, I came home from school early. I had been feeling poorly all day, and around lunchtime, I was running a fever and felt dreadful. So, I walked home. When I got there, I saw Dad's car in the drive, so instead of letting on I was home, I dumped my bag in the cupboard and headed straight to bed. I couldn't be bothered with his lectures about weakness." Will knew he had Jack's entire focus now.

"As I passed his study, I heard raised voices, so I stopped. The single biggest mistake of my life. He was arguing with a man about them having a deal, and if it was not honoured, then he knew what would happen. The man sounded really angry and Dad, he sounded scared and weak and not like the arrogant asshole we knew.

"Anyway, the door opened suddenly, and a man dressed in traditional Muslim clothing stood in front of me. Dad just glared at me and then I fled upstairs. I knew, deep in my heart, I knew this was bad news, but I had no idea how bad. Later that day, Dad came into my room and said that he needed my help. He said he needed me to use my skills to hack a bank and transfer one million pounds from one account to another. He said I needed to implicate you, or they would kill him." Will heard Jack's sharp intake of breath and looked at him.

"Why?" his brother asked.

"He said that your unit was poking around where it shouldn't be and if you didn't stop, they would make sure you came home in a body bag. At least, that's what the old man told me. I felt like I had no choice, so, I did it. I couldn't risk losing you like that."

"Why didn't you tell me?" Jack asked quietly.

"Because you wouldn't have let me do it. I knew there was a good chance I would get caught. Even then, I knew my limitations, but I would only do some time in juvie. You would have been killed if you went after them."

"Jesus Christ, Will, all this time I blamed you, and it was Dad that forced you."

"We both made mistakes, Jack. Mine was trusting Dad and not you."

"Why wouldn't you? He was our dad—still is. Is he still involved with them?"

"No. Do you remember the first mission you were given as Eidolon's leader?"

"Yeah to take out Miqdaad al-Sabir," Jack said, and then his eyes widened as realisation dawned. "That's who Dad was involved with? How?"

"He was using his job to clear ground troops from certain regions, so they could move their drugs and arms easily. He also gave them intel on planned missions."

"But why? He spent our entire childhood extolling the virtues of queen and country and yet he was the biggest hypocrite ever."

"I don't know why, I didn't ask. I got the evidence I needed against him and then used it to make him stop. He said he always knew there would be a price to pay when I was sent to juvie. I think he was genuinely sorry for that and he was trying to protect you in his own way. You were always the son he wanted. I was a disappointment to him."

"And yet you saved him," Jack said, and Will shrugged. "Did he stop?"

"Yes, I took out all the men Dad was involved with, or rather Eidolon and you did. Dad was in so deep it took me weeks to bury his shit."

"He should be in jail for what he did to you, let alone anything else."

"Maybe but I couldn't do it to Mum. I don't ever want her to know, it would break her heart."

Jack nodded his agreement. "So, that's why you set up Eidolon? To get back at Dad?"

"Partly, and partly because I knew your talent was too good to waste. You loved your job in the SAS, and I took it away. I needed to make good again and helping put the man that ruined our family away was a bonus."

Jack shook his head in shock, and Will knew it would take him days to process all this.

"So, you're Eidolon?'

"No, Jack. You are Eidolon. Everything that makes Eidolon great is you and your men. I just sign the cheques."

"Why didn't you tell me it was you, why use the voice distortion and hide everything? I looked for months to uncover who it was and never did."

"Yeah, I know. It was a royal pain in the ass too." Will chuckled feeling the hand that had gripped his heart so tight loosen for the first time in years. "I hid it because you're a stubborn arsehole who wouldn't have accepted it from me and I needed the best. I needed my big brother."

Jack slung his arm around Will's neck and pulled him to himself while he pretended to punch him in the guts. "Watch it, kiddo, I'm still the oldest and can kick your ass," Jack said and laughed.

"You mean still old?" Will laughed back.

"Still a dick I see," Jack chuckled letting go.

"So, what now?" Will asked.

"Now, we find out who set you up and get the charges dropped so we can go home."

"Are you going to say anything to Dad?" Will asked looking at Jack with enquiry in his eyes.

"Not yet, not until I've thought things through."

"And Eidolon? It can't function without you."

"I'll stay, but I want more control."

"Done. I've already had papers drawn up so that you become a half owner and have as many rights as me."

"I can't afford to buy half the company, Will. I make good money as you know, but I'm not Midas like you."

"You don't have to, you run it, and I finance it. That way I can take a back seat and concentrate on a few other projects I have up my sleeve."

"Okay, deal. Now, let's get back in and figure this shit out and let Aubrey know she hasn't fucked up. If she stands any closer to the window, she might fall through it." Jack laughed at the thought.

Will spun around and saw the blind move from her room as she darted out the way. He smiled at that.

"So, you gonna take her to meet mum?" Jack asked as they walked back towards the BBQ area where the others were sitting, whispering.

"Yeah, I think so, I like her. I like her a lot."

"Yeah, I can see that. Obviously, you're punching but women like a bad boy," Jack said with a smirk.

"Yeah like you can't get laid with all that pretty boy muscle and tall, dark, and silent vibe you give off," Will laughed.

"I do okay," Jack said smugly.

"Whatever," Will replied as they reached the others.

He sat down beside Jace and grabbed a bottle of beer off the table taking a long pull of the liquid.

"You girls kissed and made up?" asked Jace with a grin.

"Fuck off, Jace," Jack said with a smirk.

Will watched as Aubrey came over, her movements slightly hesitant. He smiled at her, and she returned it as she moved towards him. He took her hand and pulled her into the chair beside him.

"Everything okay?" she asked looking at Jack.

"Perfect. Everything is perfect now you're here," he said and saw the relief on her face before heat tinged her cheeks at his words.

"Good. Jace and I have made a murder board," she said pointing at the writing all over the inner window that separated the patio area from the inside.

Will rose and moved towards it as she followed. Aubrey had written all the details with lines to how they each might connect. It was like a spider's web that wove the particulars in an intricate pattern. "This is amazing," he complimented her, and she shrugged.

"I find it helps to have it all laid out in front of me."

"It does, and actually seeing it has given me an idea," he said stepping closer and thinking over his conversation with Jack. It had sparked a memory from when he was in juvie. "I need to see the CCTV from the embassy," he said turning to Aubrey.

"You think you know who set you up?"

"I have an idea, but I need to confirm it and see how it fits," he replied staring at the board and hoping he was wrong.

CHAPTER 16

AUBREY COULDN'T REMEMBER FALLING ASLEEP ON THE COUCH BUT sometime during the night as they searched through CCTV and looked for clues that would give them the lead they needed she had fallen asleep. As she came to, fully dressed on her bed with a throw over her, she smiled. Sitting up she saw a note on the bedside table from Will.

Gone for a swim. Coffee in the kitchen!

Smiling, Aubrey got up and quickly stripped her clothes before switching the dial on the shower to hot. It didn't matter to her how hot it was, she always had her showers steaming hot. Lathering her hair with shampoo, she thought about the case and what they needed to do now.

They needed to go to the embassy and question the staff, get a feel for Pierre and what he was like and see if anything else flagged as suspicious. But how to get in? This was not their case, and they had no jurisdiction here, but maybe there was a way.

Excitement fired her blood as she rinsed off, stepped out and wrapped a towel around herself. Aubrey began to pace as the idea formed. If she was right, they could get into the embassy and have all the access they needed to everything without any questions being asked.

Eager to tell Will her idea, she ran from the room and finding the living space empty, ran outside to the pool. She saw him swimming laps on his own and waited impatiently for him to finish.

He stopped at the end closest to her and looked up, pushing the hair back from his face. His heated eyes met hers and then she watched as they moved lower over her body like a silken caress that tingled everywhere it touched. Goosebumps broke out on her skin, and she fought the shiver that threatened.

"Morning, Brey. Is that how you greet people normally?" Will asked with a quirk of his eyebrow.

She looked down at the towel that was tucked under her armpits and barely covering her breasts and thighs. "Yeah, I didn't think. I got distracted by a plan to get into the embassy," she said.

"Um," was his answer.

"Um? Is that all you have to say?" she asked as she braced her hands on her hips and glared at him.

"Um, if you don't go and put some clothes on, I'm going to strip that towel off you and fuck you until you scream my name," he said, and she saw he meant every word.

Her body began to tingle, and she squirmed as desire pooled in her belly. The thought of Will taking her on this patio, and the passion she saw in his eyes made her nipples bead and her mouth dry.

"You wouldn't dare," she challenged and then wondered if she had lost her mind when Will pulled himself out of the water, and his firm, wet, muscled body prowled closer to her as water ran down the tattooed skin of his abs, accentuating the v of muscle that made her want to melt.

He was close enough that she could feel the heat from his skin when he stopped. Taking her hand, he brought it to his lips and rubbed her fingertips over his lips. She watched enraptured and gasped as he pulled her flush with his body until there was not a millimetre between them. Aubrey felt every single muscle and ridge against her, especially the hard ridge of his cock against her belly.

Her breath came fast, and Will traced the pulse that thrummed in her neck with his fingers. "Are you sure I wouldn't dare, Brey? Because I have to tell you, I'm five seconds away from saying fuck it and taking you on this patio and I don't give a fuck who sees," he said his voice husky with desire.

Oh, how she wanted this man, with all his rough edges and sweet gestures. How she wanted to let go and let him do all the things to her body that she knew he could do but not like this. She couldn't give herself to him with this hanging over them because she feared once she did, she would never get enough of him.

"Let's put that thought on hold until I know they can't take you away from me," she said with honesty that surprised even her.

Will stroked her curls that had begun to dry away from her face. "I'm not going to let anyone take me away from you and God help the person that tries," he said, and then he was kissing her, and she felt like she was drowning in him and never wanted it to end.

The feel of his lips, the touch of his tongue as he made love to her mouth, showing her what he wanted to do to her. His hands on her hips felt like a brand on her body as he played her until she craved his touch more than her next breath. He pulled away, and Aubrey swayed towards him, her legs weak with need.

"Go get dressed, and we'll sort this mess out so I can finally get you in my bed and show you what you mean to me," he said and stepped back putting distance between them.

"Will?"

"Go, Brey, before I forget I'm a gentleman," he said through gritted teeth.

Aubrey took the hint and hightailed it back to her room. The smile on her face could not be contained and neither could the feeling of fluttery excitement that she got every time she was with Will. Dressing quickly, she heard the shower go on in his room next door and grinned, bet it's a cold one. Pulling her unruly hair into a tight bun, she made her way back to the kitchen and found Drew pouring himself a cup of coffee. She blushed as she thought of him catching her and Will going at it on the patio.

MADDIE WADE

"Hey, Drew, you been here the whole time?" she asked as she grabbed a mug.

"Na, Jace and I went into town, so Lucy could fax us some documents."

"Fax?" she asked confused that anyone would use that in this day and age.

"Yeah, it's safer than using email if we're dealing with another hacker, which we could be."

"Ah, yeah makes sense," she replied as she added milk and sugar to her coffee.

Jace, Liam, and Alex came in with Jack behind them as he put his phone in his pocket.

"Any update on Madison?" she asked with a pang of guilt that she hadn't been thinking of her sister as much as she perhaps should have been.

"Yes, actually," Jack said as Will walked in and caught her eye, winking at her making her heart jump.

"And?" she asked.

"Blake and Reid retrieved her last night. She was tired and hungry but otherwise unharmed."

"But how?"

"When Chopper came to escort Will to Rojas, he took his best men with him, what was left was no match for Blake and Reid. They're flying her home today."

"Thank you, Jack."

"Yes, well one of us had to keep our deal didn't we," he said sarcastically but with no malice.

Aubrey looked at Will and then back at Jack. "Only one end of the deal was ever achievable," she answered.

Jack nodded. "Probably true. Now, what do we have on Pierre?"

"Not a lot but I do have a plan on how to get us access to the embassy staff unhindered."

"Go on," said Jack with a nod.

"Well, you guys do work with the Palace on foreign travel security, and stuff, don't you?"

"And stuff," replied Jack with no emotion on his face.

"Well, what if you were to say one of the royals was thinking of visiting and you needed to check security procedures for her CPO? Wouldn't they give you access and allow you to run background checks on all personnel in the building and in the last few months."

"That's a great idea. You, Alex, and Drew can interview the staff while Liam and I try and get a lead on what Rojas is up to."

"I'll run through the digital trail and see what I can dig up," Will said.

"Luce found this when she was digging through Chopper's service record. He has a brother down as his next of kin. Nobody knew he even had a brother. She did some digging, and it looks like this brother is a computer genius like Will."

"Nobody is like Will," Jack said with pride that made Aubrey smile.

"Yeah, well, the brother studied at St Andrews University but was kicked out under a cloud when he was caught hacking the Electoral database. After that, he disappeared," Jace finished.

"Do we have a picture or know his signature?" Will asked.

"Not yet but Luce will keep digging."

"I'll put in a call to the embassy and get you three cleared for access," said Jack

"Fine, let's get going on this. I want to go home for New Years," said Jace

"Fuck yeah, me too," said Drew.

"Aubrey, do you have a minute before you leave?" asked Will.

"Sure," she said following him as he disappeared down the hall towards the bedrooms. She followed him in and closed the door. He pinned her with his gaze as she leaned against the door.

"What's up?" she asked.

"Be careful. I don't want anything happening to you."

"I'm a trained police detective you know," she said with a wry grin.

"I know, but you're special to me, and I don't want anything happening to you," he said completely taking the wind from her sails.

"Will," she said as she lifted her hand to cup his jaw.

"Promise me you won't take any risks," he said as he moved in closer, pinning her body with his.

"I promise I won't take any unnecessary risks," she replied.

"I guess that's as good as I'm going to get," he said and then kissed her.

It wasn't like the last kiss, all passion and heat, this was tender and gentle and left her feeling loved in a way she had never felt before. He broke away and then rested his head against hers.

"What are you doing to me, Will?" she whispered.

"Making you fall in love with me," he replied, and she could hear the smile in his voice.

"Um, it might be working," she replied and heard him chuckle, a deep rumbling sound that she felt in her toes.

"I said might, don't get too cocky." She laughed as he lifted his head and grinned.

He opened the door, and they walked down the hallway. "If we get home in time, do you want to come to the New Year's Eve Party Zack is throwing at the Estate?" he asked as he caught her pinkie with his.

"I would love to come to the party with you," she replied feeling like a young girl in the first flush of love.

"Cool," he replied.

"Cool," she smiled.

CHAPTER 17

Will had his head already buried in his screen when Jack and Liam walked in.

"Jace is staying here in case of any unwanted visitors," Jack said addressing him.

"I'll be fine on my own," he replied feeling like the little brother again.

"Maybe but I know what you're like when your head is buried in that thing. You forget your surroundings exist."

"Fine," Will replied already submerged in the world of the dark web.

He vaguely heard Jack and Liam leave as he typed in the commands that would gain him access to the biggest information network in the world. In minutes, he was inside the database of St Andrews University, the same university attended by Princes and Dukes. Narrowing down the field, he scrolled through until he found the details he was looking for.

Rupert Pierce, mother and father deceased. Only living relative Derek Newson his half-brother. Using that information, he found more details on the reason he was kicked out. It was as Lucy had said —he had hacked the Electoral database and tried screwing with the vote at the local elections. What Will hadn't realised, was that he was only a year younger than himself. Will felt his heart start to hammer as it always did when he found a detail that piqued his interest.

His fingers flew over the keyboard as he hunted for an image of the man that until now was a mystery to them. As he typed in the name Rupert Pierce, malware and flags started to pop up around him making him divert and move around and through encrypted files. Suddenly he saw the tag name of the person who had been trying to hack Fortis for the past year and things started to fall into place. Could Rupert Pierce be the one who had sent malware and trojans into his system? He felt Jace come into the room but didn't look up, his sole intent was to find the fucker.

Using the new software he had developed, Will sent a spider out to collect all the information he could on Rupert Pierce, Derek Newson, and to cover all the bases, he included the detention centre he had been in. He sat back and waited the few minutes it would take.

He looked up at Jace who was watching him, his arms crossed over his chest.

"You doing okay?" Jace asked.

Will nodded. "Yeah, I feel a weight has lifted now Jack and I have everything out in the open," he answered.

"Yeah, he told me about your dad, I'm so sorry. If we had known…."

"Forget it, it's done. As long as mum never finds out, I'm good."

"She won't hear a word from me."

"I know. I trust you, Jace. So, when is the wedding of the year? Well, next year's wedding of the year?"

Jace chuckled and rubbed the stubble on his chin. "Lucy wants a summer wedding, but she also wants it someplace where we won't have kidnappers, murderers, divine weirdos, and general psychos so she has it tied down to two top-secret locations at the moment, but definitely next summer," he said with a look of complete adoration on his face.

"How did you know Lucy was the one?" Will asked.

Jace tilted his head as he looked at him. "When I looked at my future and there was no me without her. She is my life, the air that I breathe. It may sound sappy but it's true. My life was nothing without her in it, and now it's filled with more love than I could ever have imagined. She makes everything shine," he said and then looked down.

"Yeah, I get that. I'm glad you two found each other," Will said, and Jace nodded.

"So, you and the detective hey?"

"Hope so, she is just. I can't explain," Will said, and Jace laughed.

"You don't have to mate, I've seen that look before, you're gone for her, and if I'm reading it right, then she is for you. And no, I've not been listening in to your thoughts. Believe me, you get excellent at blocking people's thoughts when your friends all start falling in love," he said.

Will heard a ping beside him to say he had a hit and turned to see a file downloading. He turned and watched as the screen changed and an image began to download.

Will felt his heart hit his throat when he saw the picture. "Fucking bastard!" he whispered as the image of his cellmate from juvie appeared on the screen. But he hadn't known him as Rupert Pierce, he'd known him as Tommy Flowers. They had joked that his parents must have known he would end up as a hacker when they named him after the famous engineer that built the world's first programmable computer, Colossus.

"Who's that?" Jace asked as he peered over his shoulder.

"That's Rupert Pierce aka Tommy Flowers, my old cellmate and Chopper's brother," Will said as he felt all the pieces click into place.

He and Flowers had always had a love-hate relationship. Flowers was an asshole who believed he was entitled to do the things he did because he could. He'd always tried to encourage Will down the same path saying they could rule the world with their skills. He hadn't been able to see that Will had no interest in that.

"Then we have a problem," Jace said as he turned and grabbed a sheet of papers from the coffee table.

"Why?" Will asked as fear unfurled in his belly.

"Because there's a Tommy Flowers listed as working at the embassy!"

"Aubrey!" Will said jumping to his feet.

"I'm calling Alex," Jace said as Will called Aubrey's phone and it went straight to voicemail.

∼

AUBREY WAS alert as they pulled into the embassy car park. She had a feeling being around these men that seemed to always be aware of their surroundings no matter what, was rubbing off on her. Alex had let Drew drive while he talked her through a few details.

She would let Alex take the lead as she had a tendency to interview people like they were all guilty and this would take more finesse—which Alex, the charmer, had in spades.

She stepped out of the car and found herself walking between the two men who towered over her. Their heads were on a constant swivel as they looked for a threat. Drew was going to interview the technical team and check their history as his knowledge of computers made him the best option. Alex would take the security team, and she would question the general office staff.

They stepped through the door to the embassy after they had been cleared by two security officers. *Looks like Jack's call has done the trick.* The building itself was not huge and was relatively modern. The front looked like a giant red brick home, but the building directly behind was more like an office block. Surrounded by metal railings, it offered a modicum of security.

Once behind closed doors, the security was more noticeable. Four armed police officers guarded the front and looking around she could see sensors on the windows.

A tall man walked towards Alex with his hand outstretched. "Mr Jones, a pleasure to meet you," he said shaking Alex's hand. Aubrey kept her face emotionless at the greeting. Alex could not look less like a Mr Jones if he tried but if that was what he was going with, who was she to question the Ghosts of Black ops.

"Mr Clark, thank you for seeing us at such short notice. Do you have everything we requested?" Alex asked with polite yet rigid control.

"Yes, of course. My staff are at your disposal," he said as he turned, and they followed him past the second set of doors which opened into a large office.

"You can use my office for the interviews."

Alex looked around before moving to the window and looking up and across the street. "Um, I can see we have a lot of work to do before any visit is approved," he said turning to Mr Clark.

The man was in his fifties and seemed pleasant enough, his brown hair was turning grey at the temples, but it suited him. He had a bit of a belly on his five foot, ten-inch frame, but Aubrey didn't see anything, or more importantly feel any vibe from him, that kicked her radar into gear.

"Do we know who will be visiting?" he asked Alex.

"I'm afraid I am not at liberty to divulge any details at this time. I'm sure you understand," Alex deflected smoothly.

"Of course. Please let me know if I can be of any assistance," he said before he turned to leave.

"There is one question," Alex began.

"Yes?" Mr Clark asked as he turned around again.

"Pierre Aubin, the man that was murdered, what do we know about that?" Alex asked with an easy manner that conveyed absolutely nothing.

"A terrible business," Mr Clark said as he began to shake his head and worry his hands together. "From what I understand from the police, they have a man in custody that was an old friend of his."

"Did you ever meet this friend?"

"No, he was a very private man and kept to himself a lot."

"Did he have a girlfriend at all?" Aubrey asked.

"Not that I know of, but we didn't really speak a lot about private matters. The other staff may know more."

"Thank you, Mr Clark," Alex said dismissing him.

The man nodded and left closing the door with a silent click.

Drew moved closer to the door and using a small device he took from his pocket scanned the room. "We're clear," he said.

"The security here is shocking," Alex said with disdain.

Aubrey couldn't disagree, they hadn't even checked them with one of those wand things for any weapons.

"Drew, you go start on the tech team. Aubrey, talk to the office staff and get as much as you can. I'm going to interview the security team and find out why everything is so lacking. Meet back here in an hour. Any red flags, then click the mike three times on the comms, and I'll come to you."

Aubrey nodded, and she and Drew walked out together and headed to the second floor where the stairs split in two. Drew went right, and she headed left. Opening the outer door, Aubrey stepped through silently and looked around. Six desks were scattered around the room and towards the back was what she was looking for.

Aubrey headed towards the kitchenette and the lone man there. Moving inside she smiled at the man making coffee. "Hi."

"Oh hi, you want some?" the man asked.

"Love some, thank you."

"Are you the lady here to interview us for a visit?"

"Yep, that's me," Aubrey said taking the coffee she was handed.

"Mr Clark is very excited about it, we've never had a royal visit us here."

"Yes, well, hopefully, we can get it organised. Do you have a moment now?"

"Yeah, sure," he said taking a seat at the long bench that served as a table.

"So, tell me your name?" Aubrey said with a smile.

"Tom. Tommy Flowers," he said with a smile.

Aubrey felt her heart beat faster at the name but kept her calm and focused on her training and everything she had learned from Fortis and Eidolon. "So, tell me about the staff here. Any new hires lately?" she asked keeping her tone neutral but friendly.

"I'm probably the newest hire."

"How long have you been here?"

"Six months," he said, and Aubrey surveyed him. He was probably the same age as her with dark blonde hair and blue eyes. "What do you do here?"

"Just admin stuff."

"You don't sound fulfilled," Aubrey said with a tip of her head. "I guess it gets tiresome being in an office with so many women."

He tipped his head at her, and she sensed he was becoming suspicious. Using her coffee cup as cover, she lifted her arm.

He reached out and snagged it. "You don't want to do that, Miss Herbert. We wouldn't want to alert the men downstairs now, would we?"

CHAPTER 18

WILL RACED FOR THE SUV WITH JACE ON HIS HEELS. THE SENSE OF urgency he felt to get to Aubrey was like a knife in his gut. She hadn't answered her phone, and every time it went to voicemail, he thought he might puke.

"Let me drive," yelled Jace pushing in front of him.

Will happily let him, knowing his strengths lay in the CCTV at the embassy and his ability to get Alex alerted. He hit call on his phone, and it rang until Alex picked up. He could hear Jace updating Jack beside him.

"Alex, Tommy Flowers is Chopper's brother and he works on the admin floor at the embassy," he said before he could speak.

"Fuck. On it. Let me call you back," he replied and hung up.

Hacking into the CCTV feed, Will took over control of the cameras from the security team and quickly found Aubrey and Flowers. From this angle, he couldn't see a lot, but her posture was stiff even though her face was relaxed. Flowers looked a lot different, more muscled, almost like a different person but it was definitely him. He was sitting with his side to the camera, but the angle of his arm made Will think that perhaps he had a gun pointed at Aubrey.

He felt fury go through him, but it was tempered by complete terror at the thought of something happening to the woman he loved, and he did love her. He had been holding back out of respect for her need to go slow, but the thing jumping at him now was that he wished he had told her. He wanted nothing ever left unsaid between them.

His phone rang, and he hit accept while trying to get different angles on the screen. "Go," he said to Alex.

"Sorry that took so long, one of the guards was working for Flowers and tried to keep us off the floor. I can see you have control of the cameras and we have the floor secured. They aren't going anywhere."

"We're ten minutes out. Has Jack made contact?"

"Yes, and he's further out. With your permission, I'll take the lead on this."

"My permission?"

"You are the boss, Will."

"Fuck that shit, I'm not, and if you ever ask me if you can take the tactical lead again when you know you're the next person for it, I'll fire your ass."

"Copy that," Alex replied.

"What do you need from me?" Will asked as he grabbed the handrail as Jace took a corner at speed.

"Aubrey is calm which is great, but Flowers will realise very soon that he's trapped and try and use her as a shield or a bargaining chip. I need you to disable all the doors when we say. We don't want him locking us out. Also, maintain camera access as he'll try and lock us out of that as well. Oh, and I want ears in that room asap."

"Fine, that I can do. Just get her out of there in one piece," Will said his voice choked suddenly.

"We won't let anything happen to her, Will, I promise you," he vowed.

The call disconnected, and Will quickly did everything Alex had requested. He popped the comms unit in his ear as did Jace and then he could talk to Alex in real time and hear Aubrey. She began to speak, and he thought his heart would explode with pride as she calmly questioned him, still determined to get to the bottom of this even though she had a gun on her.

Jace parked the SUV in the street that ran parallel to the embassy. He could see the floor she was on from here, the window even but he couldn't get to her, and he had never felt so impotent in his life. Not even when his dad had put him in the untenable position of breaking the law and getting his brother fired did he feel like he did now.

He had to put his complete faith in the men his brother had hired. He had read every single one of the Eidolon employees files and knew they were some of the best. Now he just had to wait.

~

Aubrey studied the man who had set Will up and tried to get his measure, but she couldn't. There seemed to be so much more going on here than she could grasp.

"So how do you know Will?" she asked as she watched the gun he had produced from under the bench where they sat. He had been planning this all along. It was as if he had been pulling their strings the entire time.

"Will and I were cellmates," he answered calmly as if they were just having a chat over coffee like friends.

"What did you do?" she asked wanting him to open up to her.

"Oh, come on, detective, a smart woman like you must already know that. Don't waste my time," he said a frown pulling his face into a cruel line.

"My mistake, yes I do know. So why the vendetta against Will? Why set him up?"

"I wouldn't call it a vendetta, detective. Will just chose the wrong side, so he has to be eliminated."

"But you killed Pierre?" she asked trying to unravel the complex web he had woven.

Flowers looked at his watch and then back at her. "I didn't kill him.

I just made it look like Will did. I have no stomach for death, not like Derek does. He is a mean motherfucker," Flowers said with pride.

"Does he know you're here?" she asked trying to find out if they could expect him to turn up.

"Tut tut, detective. There you go again thinking I'm stupid. I know what you're doing, trying to feed info to your friends so that they can rescue you."

"So, what's the plan? Are you going to kill me? Kidnap me? What the fuck are we doing here?" she asked losing patience with him.

Flowers chuckled at her words, throwing his head back and Aubrey could see what an attractive man he could have been if he wasn't completely barking mad. "I can see why Will likes you, you have a fire in your belly. The answer to your question is nothing. I just wanted to meet you."

Aubrey cocked her head at his words, she didn't believe that for a second. A man like him didn't just do things, he always had a reason, she just needed to figure out what his was. Her brain was whirring with a million questions even as her nerves tried to break free every time she caught sight of the gun.

She watched as the women from the office were discreetly herded out of the room by Drew and knew Flowers had seen.

"And then there were two," he said with a smile.

"I don't get you. You're risking everything for what? Money, power? Tell me because I really don't understand."

"Poor little orphan Aubrey, always needing the answers to every question. Don't you realise yet that life isn't neat and tidy? It can't be tied up with a pretty ribbon. Life is all about those that can and those that cannot. I do this because I can, it's that simple."

"Bullshit, I don't believe that."

"So, you honestly believe that the boys that set fire to your parent's home had a motive other than that they could?" he asked and Aubrey visibly winced as she sucked in a breath.

"How do you know about that?"

"You meet a lot of people in jail, detective, and Mickey was more than willing to tell me about his exploits. He did seem to have a certain amount of regret about your parents though. You were the one that got away from him. Who knows, if his gang hadn't brutally killed your parents because they could, you two might have ended up happily making babies together."

Aubrey fought the cacophony of emotions that swirled through her at the mention of Mickey and his involvement with her parent's deaths, no matter that he hadn't been the one to do it. His guilt by association was enough for her.

"You're wrong, the fact that he was in there proved who he was."

"Like Will you mean? He was in jail, so he's automatically a bad person?" he asked.

"No, that is not what I meant. Will saved himself, he was never bad. Mickey was a lost soul that needed saving, and I was never the person for that job."

"Maybe not, detective, maybe not," he said as he looked to the ceiling and smiled. "Time to go, let's move," he said as he raised the gun up and motioned for her to stand.

~

WILL JUMPED out of the car as he watched a helo fly in low towards the embassy and hover. "What the fuck?"

"It's Chopper's men," Jace said as they watched four men dressed in black fatigues fast rope in and land on the roof. He ducked as covering fire began to hit the bonnet of the SUV from the helicopter.

Jace returned fire as they moved for cover behind the vehicle. Will leaned in and grabbed the laptop so he could continue to monitor Aubrey and Flowers. Sitting on his ass with his back to the SUV, Will watched as Flowers pulled Aubrey through the fire exit into the back hallway that led to the roof. He locked the door in front of them and released the locks behind so Alex and Drew could follow. Jace swore beside him, and he looked up to see blood on the white t-shirt of his left bicep.

"You okay?" Will asked as Jace continued to fire up at the helo.

"Yeah, fine, it's nothing," he said, and Will took his cousin at his word.

An SUV pulled behind them, and he saw his brother and Liam jump out.

"Sitrep," yelled Jack as he ran and crouched beside him while Liam took up position beside Jace.

"Tommy Flowers is Rupert Pierce, and he's been working at the embassy. He has Aubrey, and they're making their way to the roof. Alex can't get close enough to make a shot without endangering Aubrey."

"Fine, you're doing great, Will. Just keep stalling him while Liam and I get into position."

"Fine," Will replied.

He watched his brother speak to Jace and Liam, but he couldn't hear what was said. He returned his attention to Aubrey and Flowers who was using a mobile tablet to hack the doors open. He watched as they came to the final door that must lead to the roof and felt as if his whole world was about to implode.

Then out of nowhere an idea hit him. "Jack," he called. His brother turned and moved closer, so he could hear. "I have an idea. If I hack the onboard computer on the helo, they'll either have to land or crash but I have to do it before Aubrey gets on board."

"Do it," Jack said instantly.

Will began to hack and before long was inside the onboard computer. He switched off one of the engines and looked up to see the helo tilt and start to wobble. Switching back to the cameras he saw Flowers was through the door and leading Aubrey up the stairs now. The two men left alive on the roof headed for the door as it opened, and Flowers stepped through ducking his head as he shoved Aubrey at the larger man.

The helo began to tilt and spin and pulled up just as Flowers reached it to steady it. A rope ladder was thrown down, and Flowers began to climb as the helo lifted and flew away. Will reversed the commands reinstalling the engine, not prepared to kill hundreds of civilians by crashing a helicopter into the street to stop Flowers getting away.

Will stood as Jack and Jace ran in a crouch to the side of the building. Liam was already halfway up the fire exit ladder when Jack began to climb. Will had his foot on the bottom rung when he heard shots ring out on the roof above him. His body froze in fear as silence rang out.

CHAPTER 19

As Aubrey stood under the shower spray and watched the water run down her body, taking with it the blood of the man that Drew had shot as he held a gun to her head, she tried to fight the shakes. Her job as a detective had allowed her to see things most people never saw. She'd thought she was prepared, that she knew what to expect, but she hadn't had a clue.

She felt no regret that the man was dead, he would have killed her without a second thought if Drew hadn't shot him when he did. No, the shakes were from the shock of seeing another person die and being covered in their warm blood.

It made her thankful that there were men and women like the ones who worked for Fortis and Eidolon who were prepared to do what they did to keep unknowing civilians safe. The sacrifice they made was huge, and now when she looked at them all, she saw what she hadn't seen before. Each mission took a part of them with it, each kill, each horror that they witnessed.

It was precisely as Alex had described, and she had no shame in admitting she couldn't do it but her respect for those that could was tenfold now, and she would do whatever she could to support the strong men and women that did.

Stepping out, she grabbed the fluffy towel Will had given her before she came in to shower and wrapped herself in it. Aubrey remembered the fear she had felt as Flowers shoved her at the man with such cold eyes and told him to deal with her. Flowers had admitted he had no stomach for murder, but he also had no compunction about having her killed by someone else's hand.

Stepping into yoga bottoms and a light t-shirt, Aubrey left her hair loose as she went to look for Will. He'd hardly left her side since he had peered over the side of the roof and seen her. The look of relief had told her he had feared the worst. Jack and Liam had stayed behind to clean up the mess, and Alex and Drew had driven back with them, while Jace drove the additional vehicle.

Aubrey stopped outside Will's room and listened but hearing nothing, she went to turn and walk away and jumped to see him further down the hallway, leaning his shoulder against the door jam, his arms folded over his chest. He looked gorgeous, but it was the cheeky grin and saucy look in his eye that took him to devastating.

"Looking for someone?" he asked as he shoved off the door and moved towards her.

Aubrey blushed at being caught and thanked God for her darker skin. "I just wanted to see if you were hungry. I could make us a sandwich or something," she blustered as she lifted her head and looked at him.

Will slipped his arms around her back and pulled her to his front. The loose shorts he wore did little to disguise the erection he had. "Oh, I'm hungry all right, but I don't want a sandwich," he growled as he bent his head and nuzzled the sensitive spot behind her ear making her shiver in anticipation.

"What do you want, Will?" she asked her voice a husky rasp.

"You, Aubrey. I want you spread out beneath me," he responded as he pulled the lobe of her ear into his mouth and bit down on the fleshy part, making her moan quietly.

Her hands came up to rest on his chest as she swayed towards him. She wanted him so badly, and every reason she had in her head for not being with him seemed to pale into insignificance at the thought that today she could have died, and not opening herself to Will and all they could have would have been her biggest regret.

"What are you waiting for?" she asked as she heard him growl and then she was wrapped up in him as he pushed open his bedroom door and shoved her against it as he kissed her until she felt like she was in the middle of a storm and Will was her only anchor.

His hand at the waistband of her yoga pants made her belly flutter as he held her against the wall. With his mouth now on her neck, he slid his hand inside her panties, his fingers skimming over the wet heat of her pussy as he curled a finger just inside her entrance.

Aubrey writhed wanting more, her whole body burning for him to touch her where she needed him. A moan escaped her as his finger brushed against the sensitive nub of her clit, making her wetter for his touch. She twisted her head seeking his mouth, but he evaded her trying to control her. Not one to back down, Aubrey grabbed his head between her hands and kissed him hard drawing a groan from them both as he rubbed her clit with his thumb and fucked her pussy with his fingers.

"Fuck, that feels so good," she moaned.

"Umm. You have a dirty mouth, I like it," Will whispered against her mouth as his other hand pulled the neckline of her top down so he could feast his eyes on her breasts. "So fucking pretty," he groaned as he unsnapped the bra with his hand before taking her nipple into his mouth and sucking and toying with it until she was writhing under the sensations he was forcing her to confront.

Aubrey kissed down Will's neck, biting on the sensitive area around his shoulder and neck as her hand cupped the bulge that she wanted inside her more than her next breath. Will's groan filled her with a sense of power that she could make this man who controlled everything around him weak for her.

Her hand found its way inside his shorts, and she grabbed his cock, grasping the heavy weight of it as he ground into her hand.

"I'm gonna make you come so hard, Brey," he moaned before he redoubled his efforts on her sensitive clit and she felt the heat begin to build.

"Open your legs wider," he demanded, and she did as he asked.

Will rewarded her as he fucked her harder and faster with his fingers until only his body was holding her up. Aubrey worked his cock, but her concentration was on the way he was making her feel as her body began to splinter, and a scream tore from her throat as her climax hit her, sending her mind into a spin as his mouth captured hers. She rode wave after wave of pleasure until it was just the sound of her breaths as tiny aftershocks of the most intense climax of her life ebbed away.

"I'm not done yet," Will growled and lifted her and walking to the bed with long strides. Aubrey looked up at him as he lay her on the bed, her eyes fixed on him as he stepped away and shed his shorts and shirt. His hard cock lay proud against his belly, the tattoos that defined him like a work of art against the muscle and sinew of his body. Not a spare inch of skin was left unmarked by the art that covered him.

It was his eyes that held her captive though, the windows to the soul of this complex man who had crawled under her skin and burrowed into the heart she had protected with such spirit. Will prowled towards her like a panther ready to claim his prize.

Putting a knee in the bed, Will leaned towards her, bracketing her with his arms on either side of her body. "You're overdressed, Brey," he stated.

"Best you fix that then," she replied loving the playful side of him as much as the intensity.

"Um, best I had," he said with a quirk of his mouth.

Reaching down he pulled the now creased t-shirt over her head and threw it behind him. Then he leaned in and kissed his way down her neck and collarbone as she threw her head back to give him better access. Pulling the bra that hung undone away, he gazed at her before he pulled a nipple into his mouth and bit down gently until she moaned from the sheer eroticism of it. She felt her belly quiver as he kissed his way down until he came to the edge of her yoga pants.

Before she knew what had happened, he lifted her ass and pulled the trousers and pants away before he buried his head in her pussy and inhaled. The move turned her on, exciting her more than she thought possible.

"I love the smell of you." He lifted his head. "Look what you do to me," he said as he sat back on his haunches and palmed his heavy, thick cock and stroked from root to tip. The end glistened with pre-cum, and it made her mouth water wondering what he tasted like, what it would feel like to have him in her mouth, entirely at her mercy.

"Show me," she replied her body hungry for the feel of him inside her.

"My pleasure," he said as he reached into his shorts which were on the floor and pulling out his wallet, took out a condom before tearing it open and rolling it down his cock. Instead of crawling over her as she suspected he would, he crawled to the top of the bed and sat down with his back to the headboard.

"Come here," he said in a silky voice.

Going up on her knees, Aubrey moved to him before straddling his hips.

"Hmm, now that's a sight for sore eyes," he said as he rubbed his palm over her distended nipple.

Taking his cock in her hand, she stroked him and revelled as he arched his head back, showcasing his strong neck. Will was magnificent to look at but more than that, he was an amazing man and just like that, Aubrey released the hold she had on her heart and handed it to the man in front of her.

Positioning her pussy over him, she guided his cock to her entrance, sliding it through her wetness before sinking down on his hot hard cock.

"Ah, that feels so good," he moaned as he filled her.

He lifted his hands and intertwined their fingers before tugging her forward, so she fell against him causing them both to groan at the sensation they were creating. Aubrey looked into his eyes that held so many emotions. It felt like the two of them were connected on a cellular level—it was more than lust, more than friendship. Will was the man that was her missing part—the one that made her brave, made her feel safe in a way nobody else did. She could be herself without worrying that she was going to get hurt.

"Will," she breathed as she leaned in to kiss his lips.

"I know, sweetheart, I feel it too," he said and then words were forgotten as she started to move. The drag and pull of his cock against the walls of her pussy was heaven. He cupped her cheek, and she leaned into it as she moved, his cock hitting her g-spot.

His hands moved down her body, caressing and stroking until she was pulsing all over, her skin tingling from his touch. His lips found hers and he kissed her with passion and tenderness. Aubrey arched into him as he began to rub her clit, his hips rising to meet hers as she rode him looking for the release her body sought.

Will wrapped his arm around her waist and lifted them both before toppling them, so he was on top of her.

"I guess it's your turn on top." She laughed not able to stop the free feeling allowing herself to be with him gave her.

He rubbed his nose over hers and grinned. "I need to feel more of you."

"Then get on with it, Geek Boy," she teased.

"Geek Boy is not an insult you know," he said through a smile before kissing her again. Then he was inside her, moving them both higher and higher towards the peek they both reached for.

"Fuck, Brey, you feel amazing," he said as he stroked a hand over her ass before lifting her leg to wrap it around him.

She moaned as he hit her clit with his pelvis and she felt the first shocks of her climax begin. "Will."

"I'm right with you, Brey, just let go,"

Relaxing into him she let go and let the sensation slide through her. Her body shattered as her climax hit and she moaned his name through a barrage of feeling. His body went rigid, and she felt the heat as he groaned and released his orgasm into her.

Collapsing onto her she felt his quick breath against her neck.

"Fuck. I think you killed me, woman," he said with a laugh.

She slapped his ass and grinned. "I am not *woman*, my name is Aubrey," she said with mock heat.

He raised up on his elbows and looked at her. "No, you're not. You're mine. My Brey," he said softly, and her heart melted.

"And you're my geek boy," she replied her throat thick with emotion.

Will laughed throwing his head back with unabashed joy. "Yes, I am," he answered and her whole world settled.

CHAPTER 20

Lying in a safe house in Colombia while hiding from drug lords and people who wanted you dead should not rank amongst some of the happiest times of your life but as Will lay there with Aubrey in his arms, her soft skin and lush curves against him, that was exactly what he felt.

The last few days had been crazy, but he finally had the woman who was fast becoming his entire universe in his arms. He and Jack had cleared the air and were now well on their way to getting their relationship back on track after so many years of estrangement and he could now be honest with everyone about Eidolon.

There was still a hell of a lot to work out with Eidolon, but one thing was certain, Jack was Eidolon and Will was relieved he was staying. They had to talk in more depth about their dad but at least they would do it as a team. He was not the young teen anymore that felt like he had no support.

Stretching his leg, he kicked the sheet off and Aubrey moved against him, letting out a cute little sniffle. It was nearly dinner time and he needed to check in with Jack and the team. He also needed to call Zack.

Slipping out of bed, he bent down and pulled on his shorts before snagging his phone and walking to the door. Opening it, he slipped out and made his way to the pool area. He saw Liam and Drew sitting at the kitchen table but didn't stop to chat or acknowledge the knowing looks on their faces.

He guessed they had been louder than he had thought, not that he cared. He wanted the world to know Aubrey was his and he knew that one day he would put a ring on her finger so that all the world would know it too.

Hitting the speed dial on his secure phone, he listened to it ring before his boss picked up and he heard his familiar voice.

"About damn time you called me," Zack said with directness.

"Sorry, Zack, things have been a bit of a shit storm around here."

"So I hear. You need more back up? I can send Zin and K over if you need them," he said. "I would come myself, but I don't want to leave Ava right now with the baby due in a few weeks."

"God, no. Don't you dare leave her and tell Zin and K to hang fire. I think we have enough with Jace now. Did you hear about the connection between Chopper and the guy that set me up?"

"Yes, I did. Jack updated me. Do you think he's the one that has been trying to hack us and get into the systems here?"

"Absolutely, no doubt about it, but now I know, I can shore things up better. He has a certain style. I can't help thinking that Flowers holding Aubrey hostage was to divert our attention from something else though," Will said as he paced the pool area.

"I agree. Luce and Zin are working some contacts here and if we get anything, we'll send it through. How is our good detective?" Zack enquired.

"Brey is fine, especially now her sister is safe. She's coming to the New Year's Party with me. Is that okay?" Will asked. He was desperate for people to accept them as a couple and Zack's opinion meant a lot to him. He had put his trust in Will when others hadn't, and Will would never forget that.

"Absolutely, if she is yours, then she is ours. You know how we work around here. So, another one bites the dust. My team is full of loved-up men and women. I think I need to start recruiting some young'uns for the longer missions," Zack said with a chuckle although Will knew that Zack had been talking about expanding the Fortis team.

"Thanks, Zack."

"No problem, the more the merrier," he replied.

"No, not for that. For believing in me when others didn't and for all your help setting up Eidolon. I don't know what I would have done without you," he said honestly.

"You would have been fine. You're a good man, Will, don't let anyone ever tell you differently," he growled.

Will knew he was referring to what his father had done. Zack had been apoplectic when he had confided in him about what had happened and counselled him to tell his brother which he wished he'd done, but that was behind him now—thank goodness.

"Thanks, Zack, I appreciate that."

"Good. Now I have to go, Riley wants me to play nerf with him and I promised Ava I would cook tonight," he said like a man truly put upon.

Will knew it was all an act. Zack had never been happier than he was now he had his son and the love of his life with him, and with baby number two due in a few weeks, he was like a pig in shit.

"Fine, talk soon," Will said and hung up with a smile on his face. Turning he went back towards his room and slipped back into bed with Aubrey. Her body was still warm as she curled around him like a content kitten.

"What time is it?" she murmured as she stretched, and a nipple peeked out at him making his mouth water.

"A little before five in the afternoon," he said before temptation got the better of him and he leaned in and took it in his mouth making her moan and reach for him.

"Um, I could get used to my new alarm clock," she said as her hands moved over his skin leaving a trail of goosebumps.

"Yeah, I could get used to this new breakfast," he said with a smile on his face. A loud knock on the door startled them both and Will lifted his head from her breast. "Yeah?" he called.

"Put some clothes on and meet us in the living room. We have a lead on Flowers," called Jack through the door.

"Okay, be out in a minute," Will replied.

He listened as Jack moved away not hearing a thing and wondered again how his brother was so light and silent on his feet. He felt Aubrey's fingers in his hair and turned to look at her. She was so perfect, her warm mocha skin, the dark brown of her eyes that turned almost amber when she was mad or turned on, the soft curls of her hair that lay against his arm as he held her. Even her stubborn streak was perfect because it was what made her the woman he loved.

"What you thinking?" she asked and then buried her head and groaned.

"What?" he asked confused by her actions.

"I can't believe I've become one of those women that asks you what you're thinking," she moaned.

"I don't mind. I'm an open book," he replied as he kissed her nose.

"So, what were you thinking?" she laughed.

"That you're perfect and I love you," he said honestly. He saw her eyes flicker with emotion, the pulse in her neck beating fast. "You don't have to say it back, but you asked so I told you."

"I love you too, Will. I don't know when it happened, but I realised it when Flowers held me captive. I don't want to feel like things have been left unsaid ever again," she said softly, and he knew she was referring to her parents and even her sister to some extent.

"You should talk to your sister," he replied gently.

"I know, and I will. I want to start the new year fresh with none of the past holding me back."

"That's my Brey, so brave and fearless," he said as he dipped his head and caught her mouth in a kiss that made him wish he had hours of free time in bed with her but they didn't, so reluctantly he pulled away. "Let's go see what Jack has and then get shit done so we can go home," he said with determination.

Will snagged Aubrey's hand as they left his room and she shot him a surprised look, so he winked at her and tugged her forward. "Now is not the time to be shy, Brey, they all heard you scream," he said loving the way she dropped her eyes in embarrassment before raising them again in a challenge.

"I'm just going to tell them that I screamed because it was so small," she quipped as she let go of his hand and ran for the kitchen with a grin.

"You are going to pay for that," he warned as he followed her.

"Oh, I'm so scared, Geek Boy," she replied with a saucy smile that made his blood heat up.

"Well, your little lover's tiff or whatever this is," said Jack as he waved his hand at them with a frown, "is going to have to wait. We have a lead on where Flowers is, and it's time sensitive."

Will was all ears now. "Is the information reliable or is it a trap?"

"Yeah, it seems strange that we got word so quickly."

"It came from Zenobi. Siren. I believe you met her," he said, and Will felt Aubrey stiffen beside him but didn't look at her. He had nothing to hide and wasn't about to start acting like he did now.

"Yes, we all met her the other night, she knows her stuff. She told me where you were before Liam did. Drew, you spent time with her, is she trustworthy?" Will asked knowing that Aubrey had interpreted him correctly when he felt her relax.

Drew shrugged. "I'm probably the last person to ask but would say she is."

"Don't put yourself down," said Jack sternly. "Zack trusts you so why don't you give him some credit and trust yourself? Tell us about her as none of us have actually met this Siren."

"She's beautiful and dangerous. It's a deadly combination. But she's given me no reason not to trust her. The info we got was correct and I trust Roz and K."

"I agree with Drew. I didn't necessarily like her, but she seemed straight up to me too."

"So, we trust the mysterious, deadly and beautiful Siren, and hit this hard. Don't want to give him time to bring anyone in."

"So, Siren says that he's holed up in a safe house owned by Rojas. It's fifty clicks north of here in a tiny village called Paila Arriba. The place has only a few guards, but I suspect the digital security is top draw. Will, we will need you to cut the alarms and the power. If you can block the cell towers even better. Liam and Alex will take the back. Jace, Drew, and I will take the front. Aubrey, I want you to run the comms from a distance with Will. It will be just like running a drug bust but with more armoury."

"I can do that," Aubrey said, and Will loved the determination she showed.

"Excellent. Suit up everyone. We leave in fifteen minutes," Jack said and strode from the room, Alex by his side.

Jace, Liam, and Drew headed for the vehicles to check the weapons. Aubrey walked over to him and Will didn't say anything for a second but waited to see what she would do.

"I'm sorry. I expected the worst from you and that was wrong of me," she said, and Will stroked his hand over her cheek.

"I'm not Mickey, Brey. I won't let you down like he did. Never in my life have I said I love you to anyone. This means something to me, you have absolutely no reason to be jealous of another woman, not now not ever."

She reached up and held her hand over his. "I know, I'm sorry. It was an instant reaction. I will do better."

"I don't need you to do better, Brey. Just trust me to look after your heart and I'll handle it like it's porcelain."

Aubrey smiled and went up on tiptoe and kissed him softly on the lips. "Fine, handle my heart like porcelain and I'll do the same."

"But I'm a mighty, tough man," he laughed flexing his biceps.

"Yes, you are but your heart is soft," she said and then walked towards her room leaving him to think on her words.

He had hated that she thought the worst of him, but he had to remind himself that trust didn't come overnight—it was earned, and he wanted a lifetime to do so with this woman. But first, Flowers needed to disappear, and he had the perfect team for the job.

CHAPTER 21

"Can you believe this place?" Drew asked just over an hour later as they looked down into the valley where a sprawling hacienda-style home sat.

"It's beautiful," said Aubrey as she looked at the safe house surrounded by trees and greenery.

"Well yeah, it's pretty, but as a safe house goes it's a fucking disaster," said Jack with a frown.

"Who in their right mind chooses a safehouse with so many attack points? It has so many weaknesses it makes me edgy," Jace added.

Aubrey looked at the house again through a different eye, and suddenly everything they had said seemed obvious. It was overlooked by hills, it had so many places to hide. It was a security nightmare. She couldn't help agreeing with Jack. Was this a trap?

"Come on, let's go do some recon. We don't want this flying in our faces and fucking up the New Year party Zack is throwing as well as Christmas," said Jace with a sullen look which made Aubrey smile.

"You missing Lucy?" she asked curious about the dynamic between them.

"Like the air that I breathe," he said as he glanced at her.

She loved that he was not afraid to let anyone know how much he loved Lucy. She hoped she and Will would have that one day.

"Drew, you come with me. Alex and Liam, go around the side and check out that wooded area. I don't want any surprises. Liam, while you're there, set up some nasty little surprises for any runners please," Jack said interrupting her thoughts. "Jace, can you check out the ridge over there? It's the perfect spot for an ambush, and I don't want to get us pinned in."

"I was thinking the same thing, I'll check it out," Jace said and moved away to the farthest ridge.

"Roger that, boss," Liam said with a smile.

Jack turned to Will who had been silent while the entire discussion took place. Will was immersed in his cyber world already, trying to hack the security.

"How's it going, Will?" Jack asked as he looked over Will's shoulder.

Will stopped and looked up. "Flowers is definitely here or has been, the firewalls on the security are top notch."

"Can you get past them?" Alex asked with a frown.

Jack and Will looked at him sharply, and Aubrey grinned at the identical looks of affront on their faces. She wondered if she and Madison would be able to fix their dysfunctional relationship the way Jack and Will had. She thought it would take a hell of a lot more work, but then, looking back, their relationship had never been functional in a healthy way.

Madison had been wild, and Aubrey had enabled her, her whole life by covering for her. Maybe it was time to let her sister stand on her own two feet. If only it were that simple, to just watch someone you love, someone you had protected since she was a baby, fall so they could learn.

She looked at Will, and her heart warmed, with his help she could do it. She felt like she could do anything with Will on her side.

"Of course, I can get past them!"

"Don't be an asshat, of course, he can," said Jack with indignation. Will turned to his brother with a huge grin. "What?" asked Jack.

"You think I'm awesome," Will said.

"Oh, shut up," Jack said and began to walk away as Drew followed him. "Just get us in," he called back before the five men disappeared as if they had never been there.

"How do they do that?" Aubrey asked as she looked at Will, his handsome face in profile as his fingers moved like lightning.

"Years and years of training and a little bit of magic," he said as he finally looked at her and winked.

Relief flooded her at the playful act. She had been worried she had messed things up between them before they had even started with her insecurities, but she should have known Will would not be one to hold a grudge. He was the most forgiving man she knew.

"Can I help at all? I feel like a spare wheel," she replied.

She had not volunteered to go with the Eidolon team and Drew because if this trip had taught her anything, it was that she had limits and she wasn't a fool. If she froze up again, she could get one of them killed and even in this short time, these men had endeared themselves to her.

"I could use someone to cover my back. I get kind of engrossed when I'm hacking and miss what's going on in the outside world."

"Sure thing, I got ya back," she said and went to work watching out for the man she loved, her heart full knowing that he trusted her with his life. Scanning the horizon with the binos, Aubrey took note of every detail she could, listening out for sounds that seemed out of the ordinary.

"I'm in," Will said excitedly twenty minutes later.

Aubrey leaned in, the heady scent of his shower gel making desire pool in her belly. He was like a drug, one she was happy to become addicted too. The image on the screen caught her attention, and she gasped. "That's him, that's Flowers. What the hell happened to him?" Flowers had been beaten to a pulp, his face a swollen mass of flesh and angry bruises.

"No idea, but if you want sympathy, then you're asking the wrong guy. That's the least of what I want to do to him for what he did to you."

"He didn't hurt me, Will."

"No, but he scared you, and that's more than enough to make me want to beat him bloody."

A few moments later as if by some kind of sorcery, Alex, Liam, Jack, and Drew emerged from the bushes around them. Aubrey nearly screamed but held back the noise as her heart hammered in her chest.

"Jesus Christ you scared the crap out of me. Stop fucking doing that."

Alex smirked. "Can't help it, it's like breathing," he said, and she realised to these men their jobs were as much instinctual as they were training.

"Everything set?" Will asked.

"Yes, we found five guards closer to the house, and they had a trip wire running around the perimeter which Liam dealt with. Did you get through the security yet?" Jack asked as if it had never been in question and she knew to him it hadn't.

"Of course, it looks like someone has beaten Flowers to within an inch of his life."

"It was Chopper," Jace said as he emerged from behind Aubrey making her jump again.

"Will you lot fucking pack it in," she said with a huff.

"Sorry, Aubrey," Jace said with a grin.

"How do you know it was Chopper?"

"I took out the scout on the ridge, and he told me," Jace said.

"What? Just like that he told you?" Aubrey said with a frown. She knew how difficult it could be to get people to talk.

"Yeah, kind of. I read his thoughts."

"That's fucking cheating," said Drew and Jace shrugged in response.

"Okay, this changes nothing. Flowers seems to be alone, and we go in as planned. Will can handle the security from here. Liam and Alex, you take out the two guards on the right side of the house. Drew and I will handle the other two that are walking the perimeter. Jace, I need you to take out the guard that's at the front. I want this done clean and on my say so. Jace, once you've taken out the guard, you offer cover while Drew and I grab Flowers and haul his ass out. Aubrey, I want you and Will in the vehicles and meeting us one mile north of here on the road leading back to Buga. Any questions?"

Everyone shook their heads in the negative. "Right let's move," Jack said as they silently slipped away.

An unexpected bout of nerves fluttered in her belly as she realised these men were once again risking their lives, but it was different because now, she cared about them. In the short time she had known them, they had become friends to her. Alex, with his wise down to earth attitude, Drew with his gentle strength, Liam who was the class clown that hid a deeper side, then there was Jace who melted her heart with his love for his Luce. Jack was something else altogether. His love and loyalty to the man she loved had cemented his place in her heart.

All of them had taken her under their wings and made her feel like she was one of them, an equal. There was no jealousy or trying to make her fall on her face, not anything like she had faced on the force. The police force was this way, but not for all women. A lot of the men saw a woman as a threat. Treated her like she was only there to fill in the equality quota.

None of these men had done that, they judged her on her skill set and nothing else, and now they were walking into danger again.

"They'll be okay," Will said as he stroked his hand over her spine.

Her body warmed at the gesture. "We don't know that," she countered.

"Maybe not but we can't go into a mission believing anything else or it undermines them. We have to have faith that they will come out alive even when the odds aren't in their favour. But for the record, this is one of the times when they are most definitely in their favour so quit worrying," he smiled.

"Okay, bossy pants," she smiled.

"Bossy pants?" He leaned forward and kissed her cheek before whispering, "I ain't wearing any."

Aubrey went wide-eyed at his words, her mind instantly conjuring the image of Will naked and swinging in the breeze beneath his black fatigues.

"Here, keep an eye on that quadrant over there by the road. Don't want our exit blocked," he said handing her the binos.

Taking them, Aubrey lifted them to her eyes and watched the road. She knew what he was doing, he was trying to distract her, and she loved him for it. She loved this man! The thought made her smile so big that her cheeks bumped the binos and she almost missed the person that shot across behind the vehicle they were using. Focusing harder she watched and saw that it was a woman.

She had long dark hair and was petite with a slim but curvy figure. Her face was mostly hidden by the hat she wore, so Aubrey didn't think she would be able to identify her easily.

"Will," she said sharply and felt him move to her.

"What is it?"

"A woman is over by the vehicles."

"Let me see," he said taking the binoculars from her.

She watched as Will looked through them searching the area. "I can't see anyone," he said as he continued to look.

"She was right by the lead vehicle," she said.

Taking the binoculars back she looked again and couldn't see anything. Just as she was sure she was going crazy, she heard the roar of a motorbike and saw the dust kick up as the machine peeled out onto the road like a bullet, leaving nothing but sand in its wake.

"Did you see who it was?" Will asked.

"No, a woman with dark hair but I couldn't see her face."

"Hmm. I need to inform Jack," he replied as he clicked the radio. "Come in, alpha one." She listened for Jack to respond.

"This is alpha one, go ahead."

"Be advised we had visual on a lone subject near the vehicles. They left on a motorbike headed towards the road."

"Copy that. Head for the vehicles, and we'll rendezvous in eight minutes."

"Copy."

"We need to pack up and head to the vehicles," Will said as the sound of a shot rang out destroying the silence of the valley.

Aubrey went still, and then the sound of more gunfire propelled her into action. Will packed the laptop away, and she handed him a weapon. Will, she now knew, was very proficient with a firearm, but why she would have thought any different was silly. He worked at Fortis and was the mystery man in charge of Eidolon. Of course, he could handle a weapon.

He turned to her. "Ready?" he asked as he grabbed her hand in his.

"Yes," she said as adrenalin coursed through her body.

As they were running through the trees that ran down the hill on silent feet, they heard an explosion to their left as they passed the hacienda. The shock of the sound caused her to lose her footing, and she tripped, but Will caught her, stopping her from hitting her head on a tree stump.

"Keep going," he urged as he held on to her arm, practically dragging her as his long legs ate up the ground. In minutes they were beside the vehicles. Will stopped her with a hand on her arm.

"Let me check for explosives before you go near," he said as he took out a device much like a bug scanner and ran it all over the vehicles and then finding nothing ran it under the cars. "All clear," he said opening the driver's door of the lead vehicle. "Hop in, and I'll follow right behind you," he said as he dropped a hard kiss on her lips.

"Okay," she said and started the engine and fastened her seatbelt. She watched as Will did the same behind her before pulling out as another explosion rocked the ground beneath her.

CHAPTER 22

Will scanned the horizon for his brother and his men as he kept a close eye on Aubrey driving in front of him. The second explosion had not been planned, and the yelling and shouting over his comms seconds before followed by silence directly afterwards was threatening his composure.

He knew they had secured Flowers and were heading for the exit when the bomb or whatever it was had detonated. Will fought to keep his panic to a dull roar in his head as he prayed for the sound of Jack's voice in his ear.

He slowed and pulled in behind Aubrey at the rendezvous location, his eyes never stopped moving, and they left both engines running. He tapped the comms to check it was working, and it suddenly came to life.

"This is alpha seven, please respond," the sound of Jace's voice was a welcome one.

"Alpha seven this is control, come in."

"We've lost contact with alpha one's team. I'm moving my position and going in."

Will went still not knowing what to do but feeling this was the wrong call. Jace had so much field experience, but Will could not shake the feeling this was the wrong thing to do.

"Negative, stick with the plan," Will said and heard dead silence. He had no idea if his cousin would take the slightest bit of notice of him in this situation or if he even had the right to order anyone to do anything.

"Received," Jace said.

Smoke was billowing from the hacienda now, and it wouldn't be long before it attracted attention from the nearby town. He had to have faith that Jack would get him and his men out of there, the alternative was not acceptable.

Minutes ticked by and he watched until he thought he would go mad and then through the bushes walked Alex, with Liam thrown limply over his shoulder. Behind him, Drew and Jack carried a barely conscious Flowers.

A tsunami of relief barrelled over him at the sight of them all, instantly replaced by fear at Liam's limp body and the stern looks from Jack and Alex. He saw Aubrey exit the vehicle and move to open the rear door. Jumping down, he rushed to help Alex as he manoeuvred Liam inside. The bloody gash to his leg and the open compound fracture where his thigh bone was sticking out was severe, but nothing compared with blood that poured from Liam's face.

Jace ran over and shoved him out the way as he went to work helping Alex secure Liam.

"What the fuck happened?" Will asked Jack, shaken by the sight of Liam so injured and ignoring Flowers who was being dragged by Drew towards the second SUV.

"Shit fucking happened, that's what," he replied. "The place was rigged, it would have killed us all if Liam hadn't been able to disable it. Unfortunately, it also had a second, smaller bomb which Liam took the brunt of. We need to get him to a hospital and fucking fast. Aubrey, you drive this vehicle while Alex and Jace stabilise Liam. Will, you and Drew are with me and the scum bag," he said as he slammed the back door on the lead car and moved towards the second, a look of murderous intent on his face.

Will climbed in and pulled out behind Aubrey as Jack got on his phone. He glanced in the rear-view mirror and saw Drew had gagged and blindfolded a barely alive Flowers. Will wondered what had happened to Flowers after he'd left the embassy and hoped the fucker lived long enough that he could ask him why he had done all this.

"Zack, we have a problem, and I need a favour or Liam is going to die," Jack said into the phone from his place sat beside Will.

The words were like a dash of cold water thrown over him.

∼

Cunningham Estate

Zack paced like a caged beast as he waited on word from the other side of the world about Liam. It had been four hours since he'd spoken to Jack and offered his assistance. He glanced up at the knock on his study door.

"Yes, come in," he called as he lifted the tumbler of cognac to his lips and took a sip, letting the warmth seep down and warm him from the inside out. The door opened just a fraction, and Celeste walked in with Samson, her German Shephard and constant companion.

"Did you hear anything yet?" she asked as she moved towards the Chesterfield sofa and sat down as Samson lay at her feet, his back to her. A silent warning to anyone trying to get too close, that they would have to go through him first.

"Not yet, but it shouldn't be too long now," he replied as he observed the woman who had banged down his door at two yesterday morning and demanded to talk to him. Celeste Bourdain was his best friend's sister. And Zin, his most lethal operative, had decided she was the love of his life, but Celeste was no ordinary woman, not least because she had tamed the wildness in Zin 'The Viper' Maklavoi. No, she was unique because she could read people's thoughts just by touching them, but she also had visions of the future.

Those came few and far between but were never wrong, and last night she had seen Jack, Alex, Drew, and Liam walk into a building and Liam come out barely alive after a massive explosion.

Zack had taken her warning seriously and tried to reach Jack to warn him but with no luck, he'd done the only other thing he could and that was to send back up. Zin and Kanan had already been enroute when Zack had spoken on the phone with Will, but he hadn't known the threat at the time so couldn't warn him.

Zack had decided against admitting Zin and K were on their way, not wanting Will to argue against it. The thing with Will was that he didn't accept help very well, so Zack had always found presenting him with a fait accompli was the best course of action. An hour later after Celeste had managed to give them the location from landmarks that had subsequently been confirmed by Will's watch, he had called Zin and K to tell them.

Zin had secured a chopper and Kanan had used his contacts to have a doctor fly in with them from a Doctors Without Borders programme that was running in the vicinity.

"What if they were too late?" Celeste asked, and Zack saw the worry and responsibility her visions placed on her small shoulders.

The woman had been through so much this year and had proved herself to be stronger than she knew. Her desire to sacrifice herself to save so many had been admirable, but she still had a softness that endeared her to everyone she met.

"They would've called in by now if they'd missed them. They're probably just helping the team secure things before coming home."

"I hope so. I couldn't bear it if anything happened to Liam or any of them." Zack wasn't so sure Zin would see it that way if he heard her so worried over another man but kept his counsel. "Liam is still grieving for Ambrose you know. He blames himself for his death," she said sadly.

"Liam knows better than anyone that in this life things happen that we can't control. What happened to Ambrose was a freak accident."

"Maybe but knowing something and feeling something are two very different things," Celeste murmured as she rubbed her hand over Samson's fur idly. "Look at you and Ava. You know childbirth is safer than it has ever been and that millions of babies are born every year, but when the time comes, it won't stop you losing your mind with fear that Ava will be the one in pain or she will be the one hurt."

"That's different," Zack said with a shake of his head.

"Is it? Both are situations where you know one thing but feel another that you can't control."

"It's different because I'll see Ava in pain and won't be able to help her, except to hold her hand."

"Liam is the same. He saw his friend in pain and couldn't help, and now he has to watch his godson grow up without a father."

"I'm not so sure they are the same," Zack said looking at his watch again, the feeling in his belly starting to turn from confident that Liam would make it, to worry that they hadn't heard anything.

The door opened, and the light of his life walked in, her round belly protruding neatly in front of her. He teased her about eating for two, but the truth was, she was more beautiful than ever. He kept thinking he couldn't love her more and then every morning he woke, and boom, he did.

"Hey," he said holding out his arm for her to come to him, which she did.

Ava always seemed to know when he needed her close. Their bond was stronger than anything he had ever known. He fought a constant battle every time he thought of her birthing their child between excitement and abject terror.

"Any news?" she asked as she kissed his cheek and rubbed her hand over his chest.

"Not yet," he replied as he sat in his armchair and pulled her onto his lap.

She lay with her head on his shoulder as she stroked his chest in soothing circles. Her scent enveloped him, and he felt the calming effect he always did from being in her space.

"They'll be fine, those guys are indestructible," she added.

"Maybe so," he started to say when his mobile phone rang. He shifted, grabbing the phone from the arm of the chair where he had placed it and answered. "Zack."

"Zack, it's Drew. Will asked me to call and update you on Liam. Dr Knowles stabilised him, and he's now on a flight home. Liam will need an operation when he gets home, but she managed to reduce the fracture. The head wound wasn't as bad as we first thought, and he regained consciousness enough to hit on the doctor, so we feel sure he'll be fine," Drew said with a smile in his voice.

"That's fantastic news. Who went with him?"

"Dr Knowles flew out with him and so did Jack."

"And what about Flowers?"

"He isn't talking, but it doesn't matter because Will has found all he needs to link him to Pierre's murder."

"Fine. Well, get your asses back home. My wife has enough to worry about without you lot playing hero in the jungle," Zack said briskly. He caught the lift of his wife's brow and ignored it.

"Yes, boss, we should be in the UK by late tomorrow afternoon," Drew replied happily.

"Fine. See you all then," Zack replied and then hung up. He turned to Celeste and Ava who were waiting expectantly for him to update them and relayed the information.

"Oh, thank God," said Celeste visibly sagging with relief.

"Poor Liam will spend New Year's Eve in hospital," said Ava.

Zack snorted at that. "Don't feel sorry for him, he'll have the nurses falling all over him. He'll be in heaven," he said.

"Very true." Celeste laughed at the thought.

"Right, time to go to bed. I'm beat, and it won't be long before I need to get up to pee seeing as this baby thinks my bladder is a trampoline. I swear this kid is going to be a gymnast," said Ava rubbing her bump reverently, a warm smile on her face as she spoke.

"Yes, I need to go speak with Roz and then I'll hit the hay too," said Celeste as she walked out the door, Samson at her heels.

Ava looked at him, and Zack felt the ever-present pull of desire for her. "Now, Mr Cunningham, shall we discuss this penchant you have for blaming me for your worrying to save your manly ego?" she asked with a smirk.

"Or we could go upstairs, and I could make you scream while I eat your pussy?" he countered.

Ava looked up and to the left as if she was thinking, tapping her lip with her index finger. "Um, you drive a hard bargain. We should probably discuss the options in private," she replied.

Zack gave her no time to change her mind and swept her into his arms and made for the stairs. He wanted his woman, and nobody and nothing was getting in the way of that tonight.

CHAPTER 23

As the plane touched down at Shobdon Airfield, Will felt his body relax. It had been a harrowing few days and he for one was exhausted, and it wasn't over yet. Flowers hadn't talked even though they had found most of the evidence he had needed to clear himself.

The authorities in Colombia had had little choice but to concede he had been set up when they had presented them with the facts. Couple that with the evidence that the four officers who had arrested him had been working for Rojas and he had been home and clear.

There were just a few things niggling him, and he could only get those answers from Flowers. He turned to Aubrey who was rubbing the sleep from her eyes and rubbed her knee. He'd not had any time alone with her since before the raid on Flowers' safehouse, and he needed to feel her against him again.

Her touch, fuck her very presence, had become essential to keep him grounded. He needed her in a way he had never needed anyone, and it scared the shit out of him.

"Nice sleep?" he asked as she stretched her arms up and yawned.

"Yes, I must have been knackered to have slept through the landing," she answered as Will tried to tear his eyes from the way her top lifted exposing the silky flesh of her midriff.

"Well, let's get you home, and you can sleep the whole day away," he said rubbing her cheeks with his thumb, the lump in his chest heavy with love for this incredible woman.

"Will I see you later?" she asked as they stood, and he handed her the small bag she had left with. The look she gave him was full of uncertainty, and he knew what she felt because he felt it himself. Would it all go back to how it was before now they were home or were they both going to give it their all? He knew what he wanted and when they had settled, he was going to make sure they had that conversation. But not here on the plane in front of everyone.

"I doubt it. I want to be there when Jack questions Flowers again, and that could take all night," he said as he followed her down the steps of the plane to the tarmac. "I'll call you tomorrow though," he said distractedly as he saw her face fall and couldn't figure out why.

"Will," Ava said as she wrapped her arms around him, "thank goodness you're okay."

Will returned the hug, even though what he really wanted to do was go after Aubrey and find out why she had looked so upset. Ava let him go, and Zack shook his hand, a smile on his face. Daniel and Megan greeted him next as Lizzie stood with Lucy and Jace.

"Can't believe you stole your own plane," he said shaking his head.

"Yeah, crazy town huh," he replied as he looked around and saw Aubrey's back as she disappeared through the lounge door. Around him couples were embracing, and Lucy was fussing over Jace's measly bullet wound while he kissed her temple and held her tight against him like he never wanted to let go.

Zin and Celeste were walking hand in hand, her head leaning against his much taller shoulder. Even Roz had arrived with the girls to meet K, both girls chattering a mile a minute as if they hadn't seen him in months rather than just a few days.

Moving into the lounge as a group he saw that Aubrey was in her sister's arms and both were crying. Blake, who had been standing beside Madison, came over and shook Alex's hand.

He desperately wanted to go to Aubrey, but she needed this time with Madison more than she needed him right now, so he decided to give her space.

"Any word from Jack?" Blake asked.

"Yes, he's meeting us and Flowers at Eidolon. I'm going to go help Drew transport him as soon as Reid arrives with the vehicle."

"You mean that one?" Blake asked pointing at the large black van that had pulled up alongside the plane.

Everything seemed to happen in slow motion then as Alex yelled 'No!' Everyone turned as bullets began to spray the plane where Drew was with Flowers. Another van pulled up and four men in black fatigues jumped out and started firing on the hanger where they stood. All around, men started to push their loved ones down and out of harm's way.

Will saw Zack push Ava down and cover her with his body and dove towards Aubrey as glass began to shatter around them, pulling her behind a coffee machine. Alex, Blake, Jace, Lucy, and Zin dove into action returning fire as K pushed Katarina and Natalia into Roz behind some chairs before kissing his wife and running for the door. Daniel pushed Megan behind the reception desk with Lizzie, and Will saw him palm his weapon before running towards his teammates.

Will watched in horror as Zack looked at Ava who had tears running down her face as she looked at the man she loved, and with strength he knew he didn't have, nodded. "Go."

Will had never seen his boss look so torn but in the end the soldier he was won out. With a final kiss to Ava's head and a look to him which told him everything he needed to know, he followed his best friend into the hail of bullets as the rest of them tried to provide cover as K and Zack made for the plane that was still under attack.

"Will, we need to help them," Aubrey said from his left side.

"I know but how?" he asked his mind a blank as he tried to figure it out before two of his best friends were killed.

The sounds of shouting and crying filled his head as he listened to Katarina and Natalia cry. Then it came to him—he had people with gifts in this room, and he needed to use them as a coordinated attack instead of as individuals.

"Jace, Daniel, I have an idea" he called and saw Lucy run to her sisters when a brief gap in gunfire appeared.

Out of the corner of his eye, he saw Zack and K crouch behind the wheel of a Chinook for cover about a hundred feet from the plane as two of the enemy fell to the ground dead as Fortis and Eidolon returned fire.

Jace and Daniel ran in a crouch to his position, heads down as gunfire again rang out.

"What's the plan?" Daniel asked even though in this situation he was lead. That was the thing about Fortis and Eidolon—there were no egos to deal with.

"Can you use your ability to shove them back and give Zack and K some space to get Drew out? Jace, see if you can listen in to their thoughts and determine their plan," Will said hopefully.

Daniel frowned. "I can try, but there's no saying it will work, my ability control is very much a work in progress," he said as a bullet pinged into the wall behind them. Megan screamed, and Daniel's face went as cold as ice. "Fuck that, I can do it."

"It's hard cutting through the chatter, but it looks like they're planning to get Flowers out and kill off as many of us as possible. It is definitely Chopper's team, but I don't hear him," Jace added. "They have two other vehicles on route to the other side of the hangar so moving them isn't a good option as they'll crash into the hangar here. We need to move the plane away from them," Jace finished to Daniel.

"Fuck. Okay, I can try. Get Alex and everyone else to give me some covering fire as I need to get as close to the glass as I can," Daniel said. As he moved off at a low jog closer to the shattered glass, he glanced towards Megan, Lucy, and Lizzie and seemed to straighten his shoulders.

Will winced when a piercing whistle blew from behind him, and everyone looked towards them. He glanced at Aubrey who just motioned for him to speak now she had gotten everyone's attention.

"Give Daniel some covering fire," he yelled, and everyone nodded except Lucy who was busy holding on to her sisters.

With a final look and nod to Daniel, Will and Aubrey gripped each other's hands as Daniel stood, and lifting his hands, brought them down and away from his body as if he was pushing something away from him, the look on his face was a mask of solid concentration.

Two things happened at that moment, the plane that contained Drew and Flowers began to lift horizontally, and the bullets that were being shot at them seemed to fall to the ground in mid-air as if they had hit a brick wall. Daniel shoved away, and the plane that was now hovering a few feet above the ground shot back about three hundred, hitting a small light aircraft and rolling another hundred feet or so. The main body of the plane crumpled like paper before it landed in the middle of a second airstrip belly up, a long, gaping metal wound ripped through the middle.

Fortis and Eidolon continued to fire as Chopper's men began to fall. In seconds, the enemy realised they were in trouble as none of the bullets were getting past what seemed like an invisible wall and Will watched in relief as they began to retreat. In any other circumstances they would have gone after the fuckers, but with a room full of civilians, two of whom were pregnant and his boss and K out there with their asses flying in the wind, they had more important things to do.

As the last vehicle careened towards the road, everyone started to stand in relief before Will saw the crumpled plane that held Drew, and then worry overtook everything else.

"We need to help them get Drew out and call in an air ambulance, this won't be pretty," yelled Alex as he took off running for the aircraft behind Zack and Kanan.

"I'll sort that, you go to Drew," Aubrey said gripping his arm.

He turned to her, again realising what a fantastic woman she was and then cupped her cheek and kissed her hard and fast. "Fuck, I love you," he said before letting her go and running after Alex.

The plane was a mangled wreck, and as he climbed in through the gap in the fuselage behind Zack and the others, he wondered if he had made the right call.

The sight that met him would forever haunt his nightmares. Flowers was dead, his body practically ripped in two by the metal of the wing that had smashed through the side of the cabin. Will blanched but out of shock not regret, Flowers was a casualty of war as far as he was concerned, however cold that made him seem. It was Drew that sucked the blood from his veins when he caught sight of the man who had spent so many hours learning how to hack and code by his side.

Drew was covered in blood, a large gash across his chest, his arm was at an odd angle, probably broken in more than one place. But it was his leg that made Will feel like he would pass out. Drew's right leg from the shin down was practically torn from his body. A scant few bits of muscle and sinew were holding it together.

Zack looked up at him from his place where he was kneeling next to Drew's head. "Will snap out of it and help me support his neck."

Will blinked and then knelt in the cramped confines as Alex and Kanan worked on stabilising his body and leg. "What can I do?" Will asked feeling out of his comfort zone as the men went to work.

"Hold his neck steady, he's unconscious but talk to him, he might be able to hear you. We need to stop the bleeding from this wound and stabilise his leg. He's losing too much blood, and we don't know what internal bleeding he has," Zack answered in a clipped business-like tone.

"Okay," Will said doing as instructed as the others tried to save Drew's life. He looked down at the pale, clammy face of his friend and the guilt was enormous, crushing almost. "Hey, buddy, hang in there. We still haven't got to the end of season three of Walking Dead yet," Will said to the silent man. "Plus, if you don't hurry up and get better, I'll have to train with Zin and no, I'd rather go back to being a scrawny ass wimp than get my ass kicked by him."

Will glanced up as two paramedics and a first response doctor wearing orange jumpsuits pushed inside. He watched silently as Zack handed Drew's care over to the professionals, giving them all the information he could. He moved out of the way when one of the paramedics, a pretty blonde woman, gently replaced his hands with hers on his neck.

"I've got him from here," she said with a nod for him to move.

Outside on the tarmac most of the team were waiting, but Zack and Kanan had headed back towards the hanger and their wives. He felt lost as he wandered towards his friends, they all seemed as worried as he was. Lucy was wrapped around Jace, her head on his shoulder while Alex was on the phone. He started to turn around when he felt someone plough into him.

He smelled her perfume as Aubrey wrapped her arms around him and held on for dear life just as he did to her. They stayed like that with Aubrey in his arms, his head buried in her neck for a few minutes as he let the feeling of calm wash through him that she always seemed to give him. He lifted his head and looked down at her, searching her eyes for condemnation of the bad call he had made.

"Are you all right?" he asked as he searched her face for signs of pain.

"Yes, not a scratch on me," she replied and then looked behind him.

Will turned, and they all went silent as a stretcher was brought from the remains of the Learjet. Covered in a blanket and a silver foil to keep him warm, Drew had an oxygen mask over his face and the pretty paramedic who had held his neck now held a drip as they raced him to the helicopter.

He looked at Aubrey and then Drew, torn, wanting to be with both his friend and the woman he loved.

"Go with him, he shouldn't be alone," she said kissing his cheek. "I'll meet you at the hospital," she finished as she stepped back.

"Thank you, you're the best girlfriend ever," he said with a grin that he didn't know he had in him at that point. It was worth it to see her face light up at his words.

"Go," she said and shooed him towards the helicopter.

Alex stepped up next to him as they waited for them to settle Drew before he climbed in. "Jack will meet us at County Hospital. Zack is going to make sure Lauren and Dane are told," Alex said in his calm, reassuring manner.

"Thanks, Alex," he said as he climbed in.

"You did good, boss man," Alex responded as he fastened his seat belt.

Will looked at him for the criticism he thought he would see and saw none. "If you call getting one of your best friends killed good, then yeah, I guess I did," he replied sarcastically as the rotors began to move and Alex ducked out of the way.

The helicopter lifted, and Will kept his eyes on Drew who looked even greyer than before. If Drew died, Will would never forgive himself, but he would make it his personal mission to hunt down Chopper and kill him.

CHAPTER 24

The waiting room was already full to the brim with Drew's family and friends when Aubrey walked in with Madison. Her sister hadn't said a lot on the drive in with Blake, but she had held tight to Aubrey's hand which was very out of character for her.

Spotting Will, Aubrey looked at her sister and with a nod let go of her hand and made her way over to him as he stood and pulled her into his arms. The feel of him all around her was like coming home, a sense of rightness gripped her when she was like this with him.

"How is he?" she asked pulling away to sit beside him as Blake walked her sister over to the coffee machine.

"Not good, they took him straight into surgery. He hasn't regained consciousness yet," Will said as he glanced at Lauren who was pale and clinging to Dane's hand like a lifeline as his other arm seemed to hold her up.

She looked dreadful, Aubrey couldn't imagine what it was like to be in this situation, but then maybe she could. She had seen it more times than she cared to admit, being a cop meant delivering bad news sometimes and it never got any easier. Seeing the family members suffering always brought up memories of her parents and how she had felt losing them.

How many times had Madison scared her stupid, but to have her sibling injured to the point that they might die was incomprehensible. She didn't even want to go there in her mind.

"You should go home, you must be exhausted," Will said snapping her back into the moment as he rubbed her hand with his thumb.

She placed her hand over his to make him look at her. When he did the guilt and fear she saw in his beautiful eyes was crushing. "I'm not leaving you, Will. If you want me here then there is nowhere else I would be than with you," she said as she cupped his face and leaned her forehead against him.

"Thank you," he said, and she heard the tears in his voice.

"Oh, Will, this is not on you. I can hear the guilt, but you did not do this," she whispered.

"It was my call," he retorted.

"Yes, and it was the best chance we had of any of us making it out of there alive. You saved a lot of people with that idea."

Aubrey looked up as Lauren sat down beside Will and he stiffened as if waiting for a blow to land.

"Thank you for helping him," Lauren said leaning her head against Will's shoulder as Dane knelt in front of her.

"Why are you thanking me? This is all my fault!" he exclaimed sounding confused. Aubrey bit back the emotion that threatened to choke her as Lauren consoled Will.

"No, it isn't. Daniel told me what happened, and you both took the only option you had. You saved them, and you probably saved Drew too. At least he has a fighting chance now," she said as her throat closed over unshed tears. "Chopper and his men would have killed him for sure, but if he makes it out of surgery, we can help him heal the rest."

Will went silent at Lauren's words, and Aubrey knew he was processing what she had said.

"Come on, let's get some air," Aubrey said knowing he needed a few minutes alone.

Will linked his fingers with hers as they stepped outside accident and emergency into the freezing air of the late afternoon. Another hour and it would be dark, tomorrow was New Year's Eve, and Aubrey could hardly comprehend the turn her life had taken this year. Meeting the Fortis crew had been a whirlwind—lies, suspicions, plots of world domination by people who were definitely in need of the men in white coats but most of all love. Never in her wildest dreams had she expected to fall in love and especially with a man like Will.

A man who reminded her of her first childish love. One that, up until meeting Will, she had believed had caused her parents death. Yet now she knew what had happened was not her fault, it had been the actions of a group of boys who thought they were men and in their rebellious dance with crime had set fire to her parent's home.

Will pulled her into a corner of the building away from prying eyes and pinned her against the wall with his body, making her gasp. "Do you really believe it wasn't my fault?" he asked the uncertainty evident in his voice.

"Absolutely, you made a call. It was a tough one, and you saved a lot of people," she answered honestly as she revelled in the feel of his body against hers. It had only been a day since they had made love, but she was already addicted to the feel of him. Her pulse picked up, her tummy filled with tiny butterflies and her lips parted as she sucked in air.

"Come home with me. I need you, Aubrey. Even if it's only so I can hold you in my arms while we sleep."

"Of course, I want that too," she said as his mouth moved closer, then she was lost in his kiss. It was gentle and tender and so damn sweet it made her suddenly want to cry.

Will pulled back and saw her tears. "What's all this?" he asked as he brushed them away with his thumbs.

"I just love you so much, and I don't want to lose you," she said embarrassed by her tears and the weakness it showed.

"I love you too, and you make me so happy. I don't ever want to lose you either, Brey."

"You won't lose me, Will. I'm here for the long haul. I wasn't looking for this, but now I have it I am not letting go," she said.

"Well, isn't that just the most romantic speech," sneered Chopper from where he stood two feet from them with a gun pointed at Will's head.

CHAPTER 25

Will turned with his hands raised so that her body was entirely hidden by his.

"You don't need to do this, Chopper," said Will his voice calm.

"Shut up. You and your friends took my brother from me, and now I'm going to take away everything from you all," he hissed, his face a mask of fury.

His face was covered in blood, the sleeve of his shirt ripped—probably from a bullet wound. This was crazy—Chopper was highly trained, he must know that putting himself out here where there were cameras everywhere was suicide, which meant he didn't care if he got caught.

Will knew if he didn't get them out of this either he or Aubrey were going to be killed, most likely both of them, and that wasn't an option.

"You won't get away with it," said Will calmly.

"Of course, I will. All your pathetic teammates are inside snivelling over that overgrown monkey," he said with venom dripping from every word.

Will felt anger for this man's constant barrage of evil against people he cared about. He watched the gun that was trained on him, Chopper's hand was steady even in such an emotional state.

"Come on, move. I don't have time for this, get in the van," Chopper said motioning to the black van parked at the curb near the A&E entrance.

Will didn't move as he felt Aubrey grip him tighter. "I can't do that, Chopper," Will said as he saw rage cross the other man features.

"Of course, you can, or I'm going to kill that pathetic brother of yours." Will felt bile fill his mouth at Chopper's words. No way could he have Jack, could he? Surely Chopper wouldn't get the jump on his brother. "Move," Chopper barked, "and you bitch, I could get a bit of cash for you, and since you stole that bitch sister of yours from me, I think you owe me," Chopper declared.

Not fucking happening thought Will as he tried to think of a way out when it came to him. "Let Aubrey go, and I'll come quietly. You only have a few seconds before the team are alerted by security from the cameras," Will said as he watched Chopper's mind whirl over what he had said.

"Fine, let's go," he said waving the gun around.

Will walked forward slowly. "Aubrey, go inside and don't say a word. I love you, remember that," said Will as he moved towards the van.

He felt her move, and when he heard the door swish closed behind her, he stepped up and to the van door as Chopper shoved him inside. He fell face first as his arms were wrenched behind his back and zip tied.

The interior of the van was dark, but as he was kicked into the corner, he landed on something, a body he thought, and his gut froze. Urgently trying to move off the body, he twisted to see it—Jack.

His mind panicked until he managed to shuffle closer and saw that despite being badly beaten, Jack was still breathing. His breaths were steady and even as Will put his head to his chest, he realised if he wasn't mistaken, Jack was awake.

He had no clue what the plan was, but he knew without a doubt that Jack had one and the knowledge made him breathe easier. Will braced his body against the side of the van as it moved away at a fast pace, the driver taking the corners fast, causing him to fall on Jack.

Sitting up again, Will looked to the front of the van as the passenger turned to look at him. He was shocked to see Camila Perez looking at him with open hostility, her pretty over-made-up face a ghoulish mask of hatred. The innocence he had thought he had seen was gone now, and only raw hatred remained.

He felt a slight nudge to his leg and tried to stop himself from looking down as he felt Jack push something into his hand that was sharp. Camila looked away and started speaking to Chopper in low tones that he couldn't hear. But he didn't care, he was intent on breaking free of the zip ties so that he could help Jack with whatever he had planned.

He was so intent on sawing through the plastic without fumbling the sharp metal, he jumped when a shot was fired, and Camila slumped dead in her seat as Chopper swerved sideways as the tires went flat. He just needed another second before the ties were cut, but he had run out of time, and Jack jumped up, taking advantage of the situation.

Diving through the front over the seats, Jack grabbed Chopper in a headlock as they both wrestled for control of the van. Will's body was thrown across the truck, the force snapping the last of the plastic at his wrists.

He could hear grunts of pain as the two exchanged blows even as the van still moved, shuddering along on flat tyres, the sound of the metal on the wheels screeching in his ears. The driver's door was opened, and Chopper jumped out wrenching Jack after him. Something was wrong, even though Jack was fighting as Will knew he could, he was pulling his punches and letting Chopper get the best of him.

Will scrambled through the front trying to catch sight of a weapon he could use when he saw his brother on his knees in front of the van and Chopper with a gun to his head. Will froze at the sight as Chopper looked him dead in the eye.

"Time to take from you what you took from me."

"I never took anything from you, Derek," Jack snarled staring back at Chopper.

"You took everything. You, Zack, all you self-righteous pricks did. If you had just left me alone to make a bit of cash from those rag heads in the sandbox, none of this would have happened. But oh no, with the information your team gave Zack, I had to go on the run. I lost everything."

"Nobody made you break the law, asshole," Jack said calmly as Will felt his heart spike in fear at the hatred on Chopper's face.

"Everyone was doing it and they owed us."

"Everyone was not doing it, and nobody owed us a God damn thing," Jack answered.

Chopper shoved the muzzle of the gun closer at Jack's words. "How the fuck do you pricks manage to live with such smugness? Always prancing around like you're so much better than everyone else. You make me fucking sick. But now you die and then I'm going to kill the rest of your team and the Fortis wankers too, starting with Zack."

"Yeah, like you're good enough an operative to kill me or my team. You don't deserve to kiss their boots, so thinking you can compete is a joke," Jack said as he glared at Chopper.

"You fucking asshole," Chopper spat as he released the safety.

"No," Will bellowed as a shot was fired and a body fell to the ground. Chopper's brain had splattered along the road from the force of the bullet that hit him.

Jack stood and moved closer to the van as Will exited, before throwing his arms around his brother in a hug.

"Fucking hell, Jack. I thought you were dead."

Jack slapped him on the back and grinned as he pulled back. "Yee of little faith," he said with a shake of his head and a chuckle.

Will looked from Chopper's dead body to the incredibly beautiful woman in front of him and felt more confused than ever. "Siren, what are you doing here?" Will asked as his brother turned to face her too.

"Is that any way to thank someone for saving your brother's ugly mug?" she asked with a stern look.

"Thank you for saving his ugly mug."

"You're welcome," she said with a small smile.

Two vehicles sped towards them, and they tensed before realising it was the cavalry. Aubrey, Blake, Daniel, Jace, and Lucy jumped out, weapons drawn as they looked around. Siren looked up calmly as if having five guns aimed at her was an everyday occurrence, and Will looked down and shook his head. He felt like he had fallen through the rabbit hole.

Aubrey rushed to him and gripped his head in her hands as she kissed his face before pulling away and running her hands all over him. "Are you alright?" she asked worriedly.

"Yes, Brey, I'm fine, but if you want to run your hands all over me you don't need an excuse." He winked trying to ease her worry with humour.

"Wiseass," she said with a frown that turned into a smile.

"Well, that's a fine welcome," Siren said and then smiled as she held her arms out to Lucy.

"I missed you so much," said Lucy as she launched herself across the distance and grabbed the woman in a tight hug.

"I missed you too," said Siren as her eyes moved behind Lucy and up as Will looked on.

Alex stepped forward and looked like he had been hit by a truck. He stumbled forward like a drunk, pushing past the others until he was standing directly in front of Siren. Evelyn?!" he asked in a voice shaky with emotion and uncertainty, and Will didn't know if it was a question or a statement any more than he apparently did.

A look of nostalgia and love graced the woman's face as she looked up at Alex. "Hello, Alex."

Alex seemed to crumple at her greeting. "Evelyn, is it really you?" he asked his face showing years of pain that was difficult to watch.

Siren nodded. "Yes, it really is," she answered just as police sirens filled the air.

"You should go, let me deal with this," said Aubrey.

Will knew it would be challenging to explain Siren's involvement in this. It would be a nightmare explaining Fortis and Eidolon, but

Siren was an unknown. Siren looked at them and then Alex with regret before she turned and broke into a run. Jumping on her motorbike she pulled on her helmet before lifting the visor.

"I'll be in touch for my debt to be repaid," she called to Will who nodded.

Then she was gone, off into the darkness of twilight that had descended.

"Go back with Alex, he looks like he could do with a friend," said Aubrey as her old partner pulled up and got out.

Alex was standing in the road, watching the direction that Siren had taken, his shoulders hunched, his face blank, like he was in shock. There was a story there, but she didn't know what it was. Aubrey kissed Will and then turned to face Detective English—this was going to be a long night.

CHAPTER 26

It was eleven pm, and they still had no news on Drew. Aubrey was curled up with her head on his lap fast asleep. She had been amazing handling the police fall-out until Zack, having safely seen Ava home where Dr Turner had declared her fit and well after all the excitement, had gone back and helped out.

Will wondered how Alex was, he had left shortly after they had returned to the hospital not having said a word to anyone. He had seemed knocked for six by the appearance of Siren and if he had to guess, he would say there was definitely history between the two and it was probably long and complicated. He stroked Aubrey's hair as Jack sat down next to him, having arrived just as Chopper's body was being loaded onto a stretcher. He had stayed to help Aubrey, despite needing a doctor which he had waved off. He had apparently managed to get cleaned up somewhere though because he was showered with clean clothes, which was more than he could say about himself.

"How you doing, kid?" Jack asked using his old childhood nickname for Will.

"I'm okay," Will replied.

"I'm proud of you," Jack said, and Will felt his eyes prickle at the words that he had longed to hear from his hero, his older brother, for so long.

"Yeah?" he asked because to enunciate any other words was too hard with a lump the size of the Brecon Beacons in his throat.

"Yeah, you stepped up and made some very difficult decisions, and I don't mean just today. You made the right call about Eidolon. I would have thrown it in your face, and that would have been my mistake because what we've built because of you is invaluable to the safety of this country," Jack said as he looked at him with sincerity on his face.

"I didn't make Eidolon what it was, you did, Jack. Your men, your expertise, your missions. It's all you," Will said.

"But with whose money? Without you thinking of it, it wouldn't have happened, and without all of the amazing things you've done and created you never would've been able to afford to do what we've done or achieved what we have."

"Who told you about the things I created?" Will asked having a sneaky suspicion he already knew.

Jack looked at Aubrey confirming his thoughts. "She really loves you, so don't fuck it up. Women like her are rare," Jack said with rare transparency just as a doctor in blue scrubs walked into the full to capacity waiting room.

Will shook Aubrey who came awake instantly and sat up, looking at them expectantly.

Everyone stood and rushed towards him when he said, "Drew Preedy's family?"

Will knew just from the look on the exhausted man's face that it was bad news.

"Yes?" Lauren said rushing up to him, Dane by her side.

"Could we talk in private?" he asked.

Lauren looked around, and the shook her head. "No. These are Drew's family too, and they're as worried as I am. You tell us all together," she said gripping Dane's hand in a white-knuckled grip.

The middle-aged doctor nodded. "Drew sustained some severe injuries. We managed to repair the damage to his liver, but we had to remove one of his kidneys. Unfortunately, we had no choice but to amputate his leg below the knee. The damage was just too extensive to fix and would have impeded his recovery. He has not regained consciousness, and it could be a few days as he has some swelling on the brain. The next twenty-four hours are critical for Drew. That said, he is strong and otherwise fit. He's being settled in intensive care, and I'm afraid only close family will be allowed to visit," he said eyeing them all.

"Thank you, doctor," Lauren said as tears swam in her eyes and Dane held her in his arms.

Will felt sick at the thought of Drew who was the life and soul of the party having all those injuries. Grief pulled at him when he thought of his friend.

"Stop that," Lauren hissed as she looked at them all. "My brother is alive and fighting and that is not a cause to mourn. We should be positive and upbeat. He needs us now more than ever, and if I see one of you looking sad then I'll not be responsible for my actions," she said to them all, her face red and determined.

"Of course," Zack said with a nod. "Right, everyone go home and get some rest, we can take turns staying with Drew, but we can't do that if we're all exhausted."

"Plus, we have the party to organise," Lauren said to Zack.

"Are you sure you don't want us to cancel?" he asked looking unsure.

"No! It goes ahead. Now is the time to rejoice in family and look forward, not wallow in the sadness of the moment."

"You heard her, go home, rest, and then tomorrow night we see in the New Year Fortis style," Zack said and was met by a resounding cheer that shocked the entire nursing staff.

∽

HAVING CLIMBED into bed at around one am and immediately fallen into a deep sleep, Aubrey was woken by hunger. Her stomach felt like it was trying to eat itself as it rumbled. Turning over in bed, she saw that it was ten am on New Year's Eve. Will was lying beside her—his arms thrown over his head, leg thrown over the duvet. His gorgeous body was like a feast for her hungry eyes.

Aubrey smiled as she looked at him with his mouth open as slept the sleep of the dead. He was exhausted, so as much as she really wanted to crawl all over him, she let him rest while she slipped out of bed and pulling on her robe over her Garfield pyjamas, padded to the kitchen in search of food.

Filling the kettle with water, she set it to boil while she pulled out porridge oats, milk, blueberries, and honey. Measuring enough for two into a saucepan she added the milk and turned on the gas before she began to stir the oats. Then deciding that porridge alone would not cut it this morning she added four slices of toast to the toaster and pushed it down, before loading butter, apricot jam, and chocolate spread—Will's favourite, on to a tray.

Catching the porridge at just the perfect consistency, Aubrey poured it into two bowls before adding blueberries and a generous helping of honey and placed them along with two mugs of hot tea on the tray and carried it back to her bedroom.

She stopped on the threshold to admire the fine form of the man in her bed, letting out a happy sigh. They still had an awful lot to figure out, her job, her sister, how fast they were going to move, and in what direction. Aubrey had always wanted a family, but she had given up that dream over the years, but now with Will in her life she found herself thinking about it again. She didn't want it yet, but one day maybe it would be nice to have a child with Will.

It shocked her how much her attitude had changed since she had decided to let go of the past and forgive her teenage self for being naive and indulging in girlish dreams.

"Are you bringing me food or are you going to just look at me," said Will as he stretched, running his hand up his firm, washboard belly as her mouth watered.

Aubrey started and moved towards the bed. "You start sassing me, and you won't get fed at all, buster," she replied haughtily but with mock annoyance.

He sat up on his elbows as she laid the tray down and climbed back into bed on her side. "Um, well, in that case, I best be on my best behaviour then, 'cos I want dessert too," he said kissing her neck. Aubrey fought the shiver his kiss ignited and failed as goosebumps broke out on her skin.

"You don't eat dessert with breakfast," she answered as she angled her neck, so he could kiss it with more ease.

"Yeah, well I'm starting a new trend," he said with a laugh.

"Well, eat your porridge before it gets cold and then maybe dessert," she laughed.

"Yes, mama bear," he laughed taking the bowl from the tray and gathering a large spoonful of the sweet porridge into his mouth.

"Don't you turn Red Riding Hood into food for your porn-addled brain." She laughed as he almost choked on her words.

"Shit, I need to hide my stash better," he said with a wink.

"Or you could let me watch it with you." She winked as she ate her own breakfast to hide a grin.

"Oh my God, where did you come from? You're my perfect woman," he said setting his empty bowl aside before taking the tray from her and setting it on the floor out of the way of whatever he had planned and reaching for the tie on her robe. She stayed silent as she finished her food, her heart beating faster as he tugged the robe open and slid his hand in and under the top of her pyjama bottoms to stroke the sensitive skin of her belly.

"What are you doing, Geek Boy?"

"Checking you're not a robot that I created of the perfect woman," he smirked.

"Eugh," said with a laugh and slapped his hand away, "you're disgusting."

His hand continued to do very delicious things to her body. "And yet you love me anyway!" he exclaimed with a smug grin.

"Um I'm starting to change my mind," she teased and suddenly found herself underneath a very sexy and very aroused male.

"That wasn't a nice thing to say," Will admonished as he caressed her belly, slowly pushing her top until it bunched just under the swell of her breasts. Aubrey felt her breath hitch when he skimmed the underside of her breast with his fingertips.

"I'm not a very nice person," she responded and felt the sting when he slapped her ass. "Ouch, what was that for?" she asked even as flickers of desire spread from the spot he had slapped, causing heat to pool in her belly.

"For saying nasty things about the woman I love," he answered as his slumberous eyes caught hers.

Her body melted at his words. "Oh."

"Yes, oh," he replied with mock ferocity. "So now that's handled, let's talk about dessert," he said as he pushed the robe off her shoulders and gathered the bottom of her top, lifting it up and over her head. His eyes landed on her body and swept slowly over every exposed inch. Her nipples hardened under his gaze making his mouth lift in a satisfied smirk.

"Are you going to make love to me or just look at me all day?" she said sharply, wanting his hands on her in the worst way.

His eyes shot to hers, and he grinned. "Your wish is my command," he said and dipped his head to tug on her left nipple with his teeth.

Sensation shot through her, making her pussy throb with need as she arched her back as he sucked the abused nipple into his mouth, soothing the bite. Aubrey buried her hands in his dark hair, holding him close as she felt the hard ridge of his cock against her inner thigh. She brushed her leg against it showing him what she needed.

"You want my cock, Brey?" he asked lifting his head from her breast his sexy smile like kryptonite to her defences.

"Maybe," she countered not ready to give him the upper hand just yet.

"Maybe, hey," he said as he ran his hand down her belly before slipping it inside her pyjama bottoms. His fingers grazed her wet pussy, teasing her entrance before moving up to torture the sensitive nub of her clit. Her breathing quickened as he stroked her, and her hands tightened in his hair. "Hmm, seems like someone is lying to me, 'cos that feels more like a definite yes than a maybe," he said withdrawing his fingers before licking the digits clean as she watched and tried not to squirm. "Care to try again?" he asked, and she nodded. "Do you want my cock?" he asked again.

Aubrey didn't answer, but she reached her hand between them and took his cock in her hand through his boxers and stroked the massive length. "I think the real question is, do you want my pussy?" she asked with a saucy grin.

"Fuck, yes," he said pulling away to stand and shed his boxers revealing his long, thick cock to her hungry eyes.

The muscles of his abs rippled as he stalked to the bed and grabbed her ankles, pulling her to the edge as she squealed and laughed. Bending down, Will took the sides of her bottoms and peeled them down her legs so she was completely bare to him.

"Fuck, you are so beautiful, Brey," he said on a husky breath.

With a knee on the bed he straddled her, keeping his weight off her as he leaned in and kissed her hard. He tasted of honey and blueberries and Will and Aubrey let him make love to her with his tongue, mimicking what she wanted him to do with other parts of his body.

When he broke the kiss and made to move off her, she wrapped her hand around his cock. Will hissed in pleasure as she stroked him. "I want to taste you," she murmured licking her lips.

His eyes went almost black and she saw his Adam's apple bobble as he swallowed. Walking on his knees, he moved so that he was straddling her chest as he wrapped his hand around hers over his cock and squeezed as he threw his head back in pleasure. Dropping his eyes to her, he moved the last inch as she opened her mouth and swiped her tongue over the tip of his cock, tasting the pre-cum that glistened there.

"That is the most erotic thing I have ever seen," he said as he fed his cock into her open mouth.

Aubrey swirled the head around with her tongue, as Will rocked forward, slowly filling her mouth with his dick. He tasted musky and salty, and the sounds of pleasure coming from him as she sucked and stroked while he fucked her mouth made her feel powerful and sexy. Suddenly he pulled out and lifted leaving her cold and empty.

"Will?" she asked as she watched him go to his knees at the bottom of the bed.

"My turn," he grinned before his lips were on her and she bucked off the bed.

His mouth and tongue drove her mad with desire as he alternated between fucking her with his tongue and sucking her tender clit. Her legs began to shake when he pushed two fingers into her as he curled them inside her rubbing her g-spot as his mouth pushed her higher and higher towards the peak of her climax where she teetered before blinding pleasure crashed into her. Aubrey screamed out in ecstasy, riding the wave of her orgasm until only tiny jolts of heaven shocked through her sensitised body.

Will looked up at her through hooded eyes, his face covered in the evidence of her release, which in normal circumstances would render her immobile with embarrassment but right then, she didn't care, she was too caught up in the moment. Will crawled up her body, dropping kisses to her tummy before reaching for his wallet where he had left it on the nightstand and snagging a condom.

Ripping it open, he rolled it over his engorged cock and lined himself up with her pussy. With Will moving so slowly, she felt the tight hot knot of desire begin to build the minute he started to enter her. The feeling of being stretched and full with his cock was more than she could bear as he bottomed out inside her.

Both went still as they enjoyed the feeling of being one before Will began to move, stroking her inside as he gripped her hips. His movements increased in speed until he was pounding into her with delicious hard strokes that made her see stars. Her body began to tighten as his actions became more frantic, both reaching for the pinnacle of pleasure they knew could be achieved together.

"I won't last much longer, Aubrey," he said as he added his thumb to her clit and stroked the bundle of nerves as her climax hit her hard. Her pussy contracted on a pulse of pure pleasure, and she felt his moan as he spilt himself inside her.

Aubrey and Will were breathing hard, perspiration coating their skin as they lay and caught their breath. She stroked his muscled back, floating her fingers over the sexy curves of his ass making him shiver and jump. Aubrey smiled as he eased out and flopped onto the bed, pulling her into his body with a contented sigh.

"Breakfast-dessert is definitely a thing now," he said, and Aubrey began to laugh, thinking that yes, breakfast-dessert was her new favourite meal of the day.

CHAPTER 27

Walking into Eidolon felt different now everyone knew he was behind it. Will saw everything with a new light. A sense of pride filled him, that somehow a kid with a record had managed to help create the opportunity that he had.

Leaning into the retinal scanner, he waited for the machine to beep and grant him access before moving through the automatic door. He'd spent the hour since leaving Aubrey after their fantastic breakfast fixing the bugs that Flowers had left in his systems. He walked past the armoury and the shooting range, carrying down the corridor to Jack's office at the far end of the building next to the bunk rooms and planning room, helpfully nicknamed Mission Control.

Will tapped on the door and waited for Jack to call come in before opening the solid metal door and entering. The entire building had been designed with security and safety in mind. Concrete walls, steel doors, bulletproof glass as well as a few of Will's special security tweaks.

His brother looked up from the paperwork that was in piles on his desk and smiled in greeting. "Hey, is it that time already?" he asked looking at the enormous divers watch on his wrist. It was the same one Will had bought him five years ago, which now he came to think about it, he rarely saw Jack without. Will had updated it with his new software, so it now functioned in much the same way as the ones Fortis wore.

"It's fine. I can wait while you finish up," Will said taking a seat in the chair opposite and waving his hand at the paperwork.

He hated paperwork, in this day and age, he had no idea why people needed to print anything, but some institutions just did not cope well with change. As Will glanced down at the papers on his brother's desk, he saw that a few had the royal coat of arms at the top and knew they were contracts from the Palace.

"No, I'm done. Shall we grab something to eat or do you want to head straight over to Fortis for the joint de-brief?"

"I've not long eaten," he said with a grin as he thought again of Aubrey.

"Hmm, judging by that look, I don't want to know," Jack replied with a raised eyebrow.

Jack stood, and Will followed suit as they headed out. Jack locked his office, and Will knew nobody else could get in there—not even any of his team. It was part of the contract they had with HRH that Jack was the only one to have eyes on some documents. Walking beside his brother back towards the exit, he heard sounds from the firing range. He looked at his brother in question.

"Alex. He's been acting weird since he saw Siren. Whoever the hell she is to him, I have no idea."

"Is he coming to the party tonight?" Will asked.

The idea of a party that included Fortis, Eidolon, *and* Zenobi was crazy. So many operatives in one room should spell disaster, but it also spelt interesting.

"Yeah, I think so," Jack answered as they exited the building and walked towards Jack's black Ford Explorer. He would leave his car here and pick it up tomorrow or maybe the next day depending on his hangover.

"Well, I guess we'll find out then," he said as he swung his leg up into the truck.

Jack rolled his eyes. "Great. Just what I need, a team of lovesick puppies like Fortis have."

Will laughed at his brother. "One day, bro, some woman is gonna take you down so hard you won't ever see it coming."

"Not me, I have no use for romantic entanglements. All they do is cloud your judgement and impose restrictions on you," Jack said with finality.

Will turned in his seat and looked at him. "Wow, some chick did a number on you."

"Not at all, I'm focused on Eidolon and have no room for anything else. Talking of which, how do you want to play this?"

Will let the change of topic slide, his brother had always been private about things like that, so he would go with the flow. "As far as I'm concerned, nothing changes, except you have to run less past me for financial decisions. I've already had papers drawn up making you fifty per cent owner in Eidolon. I guess I can delete the voice changer app on my phone now though," he said, looking at his phone as a text from Aubrey came through.

Going shopping with Madison. See you later. xx

Can't wait to see what you buy. Love you. xx

Love you too. xx

Will smiled wide and pocketed his phone as they arrived at Fortis and pulled in beside Zin's bike.

"So just like that, you're signing half your business over to me?" Jack asked as he turned off the ignition.

"Yes, there would be no Eidolon without all the contracts you've built up. This way you get to run it without answering to me or anyone else. We aren't boss-employee, we're partners—brothers."

"Thank you, Will," Jack said seriously, his face pensive.

"What?" Will asked knowing his brother was stewing on something.

"I got a call from Mum, she wants us to go over for dinner next week. Dad is home, and she thought it would be nice."

"I see. Well, we should go for Mum's sake," Will finished knowing his brother wouldn't like it.

"I just can't even bear to look at him. I want to kill him for what he did to you, to us both," Jack said looking pained.

"I know. I get it, but you have to try. Mum would be crushed if she knew," he said looking out of the windscreen as a light rain began to fall.

"I will. I just need some more time to process it all before I face him," Jack said.

"Fine. I'll take Aubrey to meet Mum then, you can pretend you're on a mission," Will sighed.

"No, no, you've handled enough on your own. We do this together, and I'll control my impulse to murder the man who fathered us."

"Good plan," Will said as he grinned. "Now, let's get going. I want to visit Drew before the party tonight," he said sobering at the thought.

"Any news?" Jack asked as they moved towards the door and Will let them both in.

"He regained consciousness about six am for a few moments but went back to sleep. But this time it was the pain drugs that did it, not his injuries."

"Poor guy. I like Drew he had, has a lot of potential."

"Yeah, he does. He has wicked computer skills and picks things up really easily, and on top of that, he's a good guy, with good morals."

"Do you think he would want a job with Eidolon as our computer guy as you refuse to work with us?" Jack said as they entered the conference room that was already full.

"Maybe. When he feels better you could ask him, but you'll have to get past Zack first," Will said throwing his brother under the bus.

"Get past me for what?" Zack asked from where he stood pouring coffee into a mug.

"Jack is going to try and poach Drew for the computer systems,"

Will said as Jack sat down just as Alex moved into the room, his hair wet from the rain by the looks of him.

"Fucking try it," Zack growled at Jack. There was no heat in it, but the warning was still real.

"Fine, let's wait and see what happens," Jack replied without saying yes or no which nobody missed.

"Right, now everyone's here, let's get started. I promised Ava I would help with the decorations for tonight and getting on her wrong side is not how I plan to start my New Year," Zack said as everyone quieted down.

"First things first, an update on Drew as of an hour ago. He's awake and stable. He has been given the news about his leg but as you can imagine has not fully taken it in given the drugs they have him on. I have reassured Lauren that she has our full support with his recovery and Will has very kindly offered to pay for a private rehabilitation centre when he comes out, so we can get him back to fully fit which we all know is important to Drew."

People turned to Will, and he hated the attention but knew people wanted to acknowledge his contribution.

"Liam has been moved into a private room beside Drew thanks to Doc Turner, and Lauren and Dane have decided to spend New Year's with them which we respect. Now as you all know this shitstorm in Colombia has a few loose ends which I'm happy to say I can clear up a few of them but first I would like to hand over to Jack," Zack said giving Jack the floor as he sat down.

"Thanks, Zack," he said standing. "To clear up any confusion, I met with Siren after the hangar was attacked. I knew Chopper was tailing me, and we didn't want to involve anyone else given the risky situation. The plan was to let me get caught and when he had taken me where he wanted, to call in back up. As it turned out, he wanted Will too. Siren followed at a distance using the tracker on my watch. She was then able to intercept the van, and you know the rest."

"How did you know how to contact Siren? You never mentioned her before," Alex asked with suspicion.

"Roz called, it was her idea."

"Let me get this straight, you and Roz worked together?" Alex asked disbelievingly.

"Yes, even I can play nice when the need arises," Jack said through gritted teeth.

"What about Camila? What was her involvement?" asked Jace.

"She was in love with Flowers. She agreed to help them trap Will using Pierre as the bait."

"Poor Pierre," said Lucy.

"So, what was his beef with you, Will?" Lucy asked.

Will shrugged. "Difficult to say. I think it was plain jealousy. He saw the relationship between his brother and Fortis and my involvement and saw an opportunity to get revenge because I wouldn't join him on his mission to cause mayhem on a global scale."

"Do we know who set the bomb?" Zin asked.

"Yes, CCTV shows it was Camila Perez," said Zack.

"That makes no sense. Why would she kill the guy she professes to love?" asked Will.

"Because, her uncle told her that Flowers had been flirting with Aubrey when he held her captive, and Camila Perez was as nutty as they came," replied Roz.

"How do you know this?" Jack asked suspiciously.

"Ask me no questions, and I'll tell you no lies," she smirked proving the truce was over between Eidolon and Zenobi.

"That doesn't answer the question about why Flowers was beaten and why she was with Chopper," Zack said with a frown.

"Actually, it does. Camila thought she had been betrayed and had two of her uncle's men beat Flowers for his betrayal, but Chopper was never aware of that so when she begged him to take her to the UK, he felt responsible for her and believed she and his brother were together still," Roz finished. Nobody bothered asking how she knew this time, they just accepted it.

"So, are we going to address the elephant in the room?" Kanan asked.

"You mean the fact that bullets were pinging off the building instead of going through?" Jace asked.

"Yeah," K replied.

Will stayed silent. He had nothing. He had given the CCTV to Zack and had watched it a hundred times while he waited at the hospital and still, he had no clue how it had happened or indeed what had happened.

"Looks like someone has an ability they aren't owning up to or don't know about," Zack said carefully giving anyone that wanted it the time to speak up.

"I actually have a theory about this," said Jace turning to Will. "Can you pull the footage up for us?"

"Sure," Will said sitting up straighter and pulling his laptop towards him. He keyed up the footage and hit play. They could all see as the shooting began and people dove for cover as Fortis and Eidolon returned fire.

"Now slow it here," Jace said as Daniel walked towards the doors after speaking to him and Jace. "Watch what happens here," he said pointing to where Lucy, Megan, and Lizzie were huddled together. In slow motion he watched the girls grip each other's hands forming a perfect circle. As the circle was made, the bullets stopped at the exact same moment.

"See it," Jace asked looking up.

"Are you saying that when Lucy, Meg, and Lizzie touch they form some sort of force field?" Will asked carefully, his mind not quite taking it in.

"I'm not saying anything, I just know that when they're together and touch, something always happens."

"But none of us have any gifts," said Lucy slowly.

Jace turned to her. "I know but remember the prophecy the Divine Crazies were talking about? It spoke of the Divine sisters," he finished as he took her hand.

"And you think that's us?" she asked incredulously.

"Maybe, why not? It all fits, and there's one way to find out. We do an experiment to see if it happens again."

"Um I'm not sure, let me talk to Megan and Lizzie first."

"Of course," Jace finished.

"If this is the case, it's big news. But it can all wait until next year. I for one am done with crazy people trying to kill us. I want to go home and get ready for the party and bring this New Year in, in style," said Zack as he looked around the room.

"Hoofuckingya," said Daniel standing. "See you later." And with that, he was gone as the others started to follow his lead.

Will turned to Jack. "Can I catch a lift to the hospital?"

"Sure, I'm going to see Liam anyway. Hopefully, none of the nurses have strangled or neutered him before I get there," he said with a frown.

"Lighten up, bro, it's time to down a few drinks, break out the funky chicken dance moves, and enjoy yourself."

Will was still laughing as they left Fortis for the final time that year.

EPILOGUE

As they walked into the magnificent ballroom at the Cunningham Estate, Aubrey couldn't help but gasp and stare in delight. The entire room looked like a magical wonderland. Beautiful ice-white swaging adorned the ceiling and the outer walls, with fairy lights strung throughout.

High tables with gorgeous displays of winter white roses with pinecones, evergreen, and cranberries were dotted around. A large bar was at the far end with a glass front and back panel that reflected the lights from above.

"Wow, this is stunning," she said, gripping Will's arm with glee as she looked around at everyone dressed in their finest. All the men wore tuxedos, and the ladies wore sexy, elegant gowns. It had taken her an age to find the right dress, but it had been nice to spend some time with Madison.

She and her sister had talked, and she had agreed to back off and let Madison make her own way in the world which had come as somewhat of a shock to her sister and not entirely a happy one if she wasn't mistaken. It made her wonder if having her ready to catch her every time she cocked up had enabled her sister to be so reckless.

Madison, although only a few years younger than her at twenty-seven, had a lot of growing up to do. Aubrey didn't think it would happen soon, but she truly believed in her heart that she would get there. She had even talked about going back to college and finishing her degree in pharmaceuticals.

"Yes, it really is," Will said, and Aubrey looked up at the tone of his voice and blushed deep at the sensual appreciation she saw there. He had not kept his hands off her since he had picked her up and he had told her at least five times how beautiful she looked.

Aubrey felt beautiful when she was with him, not like the dowdy cop she actually was. Not that she minded, she loved her job, but it was nice to feel glamorous for a change. The dress she had finally decided on was a sleeveless champagne beaded silk sheath dress with a high slash neckline. Split to the mid-thigh, it gave her free movement and added a touch of sexiness to the otherwise modest dress. Her hair was pinned up in an elegant chignon, and her shoes, her one real luxury in life, were black satin pumps she had found in a boutique in Paris a few years ago with a clutch to match.

"Let's get a drink and say hi," said Will with a wink.

He looked absolutely delicious in a tux. She thought he looked best in a plain white t-shirt and jeans, but this tux, the way it fit across his chest, with his hair slicked back off his face, the tattoos on his neck peeking out the top made him look like the sexiest fucking bad boy she had ever imagined. The thought made her smile because he was all hers.

He placed his arm at the base of her spine, just above her butt as they walked to the bar making her shiver in anticipation of what was to come later tonight. He had already whispered what he wanted to do to her while she kept her dress on as they drove here in the limo he had hired. It had taken every ounce of control not to just let him go ahead and do it in the car, but she was looking forward to this. There first official outing as a couple.

"Will, Aubrey, great to see you," said Celeste as they moved up next to her and Zin at the bar.

Celeste looked stunning in a sexy green off-the-shoulder gown of lace. Zin was equally handsome in that dangerous, slightly scary way that made her wonder how the hell Celeste relaxed around such dark energy, but it was apparent to anyone with eyes that he adored her and would do anything for her.

"Lovely to see you too," Aubrey said as she kissed Celeste on the cheek. "You look gorgeous," she added.

"So, do you, I love that colour on you," Celeste said.

"Thanks, it only took me four hours to find the perfect dress," she laughed.

"Well, it looks great. Have you met everyone yet?" Celeste asked looking around and obviously spotting a few people she wanted to talk too.

"No, but you go ahead, Will and I are going to get a drink."

Celeste smiled at them as they moved away.

"Vodka and cranberry?" Will asked.

"Yes, please," she said as she watched the stunning women of Zenobi walk in and blend into the crowd.

They were magnificent but then so were the men of Eidolon who had walked in just before them. Stunningly handsome men who would make any normal woman swoon at the sight of them all done up in their tuxedoes. She spotted Alex who was standing at the far side of the room with a drink in his hand watching the French doors and the woman who stood there in a dark red dress. Her black hair was swept to the side and cascaded down her neck showing off the daringly low back of the dress that skimmed her ass. *Siren!* Again, Aubrey wondered what the story was there but knew it was not her business. That didn't mean she wouldn't keep her eye out—after all, Alex was her friend.

∼

ALEX MARTINEZ STOOD WATCHING the woman he had loved since they were six years old as she laughed and chatted with Zack and Ava. She had changed so much and yet hardly at all. She was still the most beautiful woman he had ever met, still had that dimple in her left cheek when she smiled, still quirked her head the way he loved when she was listening to someone, and yet she was not the same.

The woman he had loved had been soft and gentle and wouldn't hurt a fly much less kill a man in cold blood and then walk away. Evelyn had disappeared a little under fifteen years ago, taken from their village on the same night he had proposed and had never been seen again.

He had spent years searching for her with no luck and then suddenly, she popped into his life from nowhere throwing him into chaos. It made him inexplicably angry that she seemed so unaffected. As if what they'd had was insignificant, worthless, when he'd spent his adulthood pining for her, missing her goofy laugh and the way she made him feel.

But Siren as she was now, acted as if he was nobody and nothing to her, and yet he still felt his body stir every time he caught sight of her. Alex took a swig of his gin and tonic and then slammed the glass down, almost smashing it as she flirted with Gunner. He needed another fucking drink. He stalked to the bar and felt eyes on him as he passed by them, deliberately ignoring them all.

"Alex!"

Fuck, her voice, the way she said his name made his body ache to touch her, to make her remember how it had been between them when they were barely seventeen. Even after all this time, he could hear the sweet sound of her voice as she came, her hands clinging to him, a look of love so intense in her eyes that it almost blinded him.

"Please, Alex," she said and the scent she had always worn, vanilla and jasmine wrapped around his senses like a drug holding him immobile.

Stiffening his stance, he turned around. "What can I do for you, Siren?" he asked his voice cold.

"I just wanted to say how well you look and it's really good to see you," she said looking injured at his curt tone.

"Really? After fifteen years of me believing you were dead, you want to make nice?" he spat with derision and saw her flinch.

"Look, I know you're angry, but I missed you," she said reaching out to touch his arm.

The touch sent a thousand tiny electrical pulses through his arm as memories flooded him. Hurt and anger doused them in cold water as he shook off her hand. "I'm not angry, and honestly, I hardly thought about you," he said hitting out and knowing he had scored a direct hit when she stiffened.

"Fine, if that is how you want to play it, fine, but I had my reasons for doing what I did. Looks like both of us changed. You used to be the sweetest, most wonderful man I knew and now you're an arrogant, hurtful prick like all the rest. I'm sorry to have bothered you," she said as colour rose on her cheeks.

He watched trying to decide what to do, annoyed with how turned on he was by her fury as she walked away. Like a fool, he let her go.

~

"Ten minutes to midnight and I just want to say a few words before the clock strikes, and we all get too drunk," Zack shouted from the front of the ballroom as he stood beside Jack and Roz. "It has been a very tough year for many of us with some massive highs and some devastating lows but what has endured throughout is the sense of family that these three incredible teams have achieved.

"I want to thank you all for your support both personally and at work and wish you all a very happy, healthy, and prosperous New Year." Zack raised his glass in a toast. "To friends, family, and absent friends," Zack said as he kissed his wife.

Will looked at Aubrey. "To friends, family, absent friends, and love," he said clinking glasses.

Aubrey gasped as Will did something she was not expecting. Falling to one knee, he took her hand in his. Her heart began to hammer as she looked at him, ignoring the curious glances around her as he produced a small box from his jacket pocket. "Aubrey, meeting you has changed my life in so many ways and every one of them has been for the better," he began as her eyes filled with tears. "I never want to spend another night without you. Will you make me the happiest man alive and move in with me?" he said as he opened the box to reveal a door key with a silver heart keyring attached.

Aubrey burst into laughter as her body relaxed. She loved Will with all her heart, but she didn't think they were ready for marriage just yet but living together, that she could do. "Does it come with breakfast-dessert every morning?" she asked with a tilt of her head.

"The full breakfast-dessert selection of your choice," he said with a wink that made her belly flutter.

"In that case, I would love to move in with you," she said as he stood to ruckus applause from those around them making her blush and hide her head in his neck as he took her in his arms and held her close.

Aubrey took the key he offered and slipped it in her clutch bag before holding her glass up. "To us," she said with a smile that melted his heart.

Will lowered his head and kissed her as people began to count down to midnight.

Ten

Nine

Eight

Seven

Six

Five

Four

Three

Two

"Happy New Year," they all chorused as Will continued to kiss the woman in his arms, sounds of singing began as Auld Lang Syne played out.

Will lifted his head and looked at the woman who had shown him what real love was and smiled. "Happy New Year, Brey."

"Happy New Year, Will," she said with a smile as she pulled him down for a kiss that made him forget about anything else.

SNEEK PEEK: ALEX

AN EIDOLON BLACK OPS NOVEL: BOOK 1

The cold bit at his cheeks as sleet and rain pelted his skin, and Alex welcomed it. The cold weather matched his mood. Valentine's Day was coming up, and as per usual his thoughts were on Evelyn. What was different was they weren't on the Evelyn of his memories. No. His thoughts were on the sexy woman who had walked away from him on New Year's Eve and hadn't looked back.

He hunched into his coat as he checked his watch when it bleeped. A call from Jack at this time of night meant only one thing—a mission had come in, and he thanked God for it. He needed the distraction despite the fact he had only just gotten back from a shit storm in Syria. His body may be tired, but his mind needed to keep busy, so he wouldn't give in to the anger and feelings that pummelled him.

He diverted from his early morning walk, one that was becoming a regular thing now his insomnia had hit an all-time high. A few hours a night was all his body granted him before dreams of a woman screaming and haunted eyes merged, so that all he saw was visions of Evelyn, bruised and looking like a broken doll, swimming in front of him.

He had no clue what the dreams meant, he had never seen her in such a way, but every time he woke, he couldn't shake the feelings of grief and anger that he hadn't saved her. Punching in the code at the front gate of Eidolon, he then put his eye up to the scanner and walked through as the gate slid back allowing him entry.

At four-thirty in the morning, the place was dark from the outside, but he knew Jack was in his office. The man practically lived there, not that he was judging, his life was just as sad these days. Not bothering to stop for coffee knowing Jack would have some, he made his way straight for his boss's office and knocked on the door.

"Come in," Jack called. Alex opened the door, and Jack looked up at him from his seat at the desk. "That was quick," Jack commented as Alex walked to the side table along the wall where Jack always kept the coffee pot.

"Yeah, I was out for a walk," he replied noncommittally

"At four-thirty in the morning?"

"Yeah, I couldn't sleep, you know how it is," he replied hoping Jack got the hint he didn't want to talk about this.

"Hmm," Jack said and then pulled a file from his desk.

As Alex sat, he saw the Palace seal on the front and knew this was a very sensitive job.

"I have a job for you, it's highly sensitive and will involve a lot of finesse from a diplomatic standpoint. I also believe there has been a mistake and that's why I'm trusting only you with this."

"What is the job?" Alex asked not fazed by Jack's words—it wouldn't be the first time they had handled such a sensitive job.

"Before I tell you, I need to know you have your head on straight. This is going to be the first time that I'm going to try and save the intended target rather than simply taking them out," Jack said holding the file close to him.

Now Alex was intrigued. He sat back and rested his ankle on his knee as he watched Jack for a clue but got nothing. The man was the absolute master at hiding his feelings. "My head is on fine, and I resent the implication," he replied coldly not liking what Jack was suggesting.

"Keep your hair on, I have my reasons," he answered as he pushed the file towards Alex but kept his hand on it. "This is the target. Your job is to protect and disprove the allegations made against them," he said with a frown.

"Why would we do that?"

"Because I owe them a debt and this me repaying that debt," Jack answered letting go of the file, so Alex could open it.

Lifting the file, Alex had the strangest sensation that opening it would alter the course of his life forever.

Slowly he flipped open the file and barely held back the gasp as he saw the face of the woman who had haunted his dreams for the last fifteen years—Evelyn Garcia was his target.

To download and read the prologue and first chapter of Alex's book, click or copy and paste this link.
  https://dl.bookfunnel.com/dme7jjocep

BOOKS BY MADDIE WADE

FORTIS SECURITY

Healing Danger (Dane and Lauren)

Stolen Dreams (Nate and Skye)

Love Divided (Jace and Lucy)

Secret Redemption (Zack and Ava)

Broken Butterfly (Zin and Celeste)

Arctic Fire (Kanan and Roz)

Phoenix Rising (Daniel and Megan)

Nate & Skye Wedding Novella

Digital Desire (Will and Aubrey)

Paradise Ties: A Fortis Wedding Novella (Jace and Lucy & Dane and Lauren)

Wounded Hearts (Drew and Mara)

Scarred Sunrise (Smithy and Lizzie)

Zin and Celeste: A Fortis Family Christmas

Fortis Boxset 1 (Books 1-3)

Fortis Boxset 2 (Books 4-7.5

EIDOLON

Alex

Blake

Reid

Liam

Mitch

Gunner

Waggs

Jack

Lopez

∼

ALLIANCE AGENCY SERIES (CO-WRITTEN WITH INDIA KELLS)

Deadly Alliance

Knight Watch

Hidden Obsession

Lethal Justice

Innocent Target

∼

RYOSHI DELTA (PART OF SUSAN STOKER'S POLICE AND FIRE: OPERATION ALPHA WORLD)

Condor's Vow

Sandstorm's Promise

Hawk's Honor

Omega's Oath

∼

TIGHTROPE DUET

Tightrope One

Tightrope Two

ANGELS OF THE TRIAD
01 Sariel

OTHER WORLDS

Keeping Her Secrets *Suspenseful Seduction World* (Samantha A. Cole's World)
Finding English *Police and Fire: Operation Alpha* (Susan Stoker's world)

ABOUT THE AUTHOR

Contact Me

If stalking an author is your thing and I sure hope it is then here are the links to my social media pages.

If you prefer your stalking to be more intimate, then my group Maddie's Minxes will welcome you with open arms.

General Email: info.maddiewade@gmail.com
Email: maddie@maddiewadeauthor.co.uk
Website: http://www.maddiewadeauthor.co.uk
Facebook page: https://www.facebook.com/maddieuk/
Facebook group: https://www.facebook.com/groups/546325035557882/
Amazon Author page: amazon.com/author/maddiewade
Goodreads: https://www.goodreads.com/author/show/14854265.Maddie_Wade
Bookbub: https://partners.bookbub.com/authors/3711690/edit
Twitter: @mwadeauthor
Pinterest: @maddie_wade
Instagram: Maddie Author

Printed in Great Britain
by Amazon